"McCabe Foxe!"

The feel of his body under her hands was wildly disturbing, and keeping him from knowing that was becoming impossible.

"I think you'd better give Andy back the ring," McCabe commented.

"Of all the horribly conceited men," Wynn began, glaring down at him, "to think you can come walking back into my life out of the clear blue and start taking over."

He smiled slowly, mockingly. "But that's exactly what I'm going to do, honey. And you're going to let me. Before I leave Redvale again, you're going to belong to me from your green eyes down to your toes. All of you. In ways you've never dreamed."

"You just keep right on hoping, McCabe," she said icily. "I love Andy."

"Sure you do. Like a brother." He lifted his head and smiled slowly. "But you want me, Wynn."

DIANA PALMER

ROOMFUL OF ROSES

MIRA

ISBN 1-55166-418-6

ROOMFUL OF ROSES

Copyright © 1984 by Diana Palmer.

All rights reserved. Except for use in any review, the reproduction or
utilization of this work in whole or in part in any form by any electronic,
mechanical or other means, now known or hereafter invented, including
xerography, photocopying and recording, or in any information storage or
retrieval system, is forbidden without the written permission of the publisher,
MIRA Books, 225 Duncan Mill Road, Don Mills, Ontario, Canada M3B 3K9.

All characters in this book have no existence outside the imagination of the
author and have no relation whatsoever to anyone bearing the same name
or names. They are not even distantly inspired by any individual known or
unknown to the author, and all incidents are pure invention.

MIRA and the star colophon are registered trademarks of MIRA Books.

Printed in U.S.A.

ROOMFUL OF
ROSES

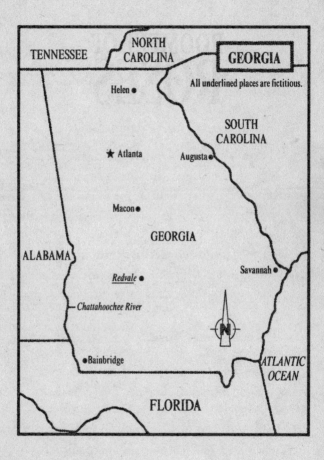

Chapter One

It was the most wonderful kind of spring day—warm after the recent rain, with butterflies gliding around a puddle beside the porch of the weathered old country store in southern Creek County. Camellias were blooming profusely, their pink and red blossoms stark against the deep, shiny green of the leaves that framed their delicate faces. A dusty road led off beside the worn wood building, and a tractor could be heard breaking ground nearby.

Wynn Ascot left her camera and equipment on the back seat of her Volkswagen and slid out of her yellow sweater before she went up the cracked concrete steps onto the dusty porch and through the screen door. The store smelled of bananas and onions; overhead was a fan that whirred softly amid the homely clutter of groceries. Wynn shook back her long dark hair and lifted its weight as she walked into the store, feeling the heat abate. The swirling blue-patterned cotton skirt was cool enough, but she was wearing a long-sleeved white blouse with it—she hadn't expected the day to heat up this much! The suede boots were just about as confining as the blouse, making her long legs hotter.

Mrs. Baker was leaning over the dark wood counter next to a cheese hoop, talking to old Mr. Sanders. But she looked up when she spotted Wynn.

"Loafing, huh?" the white-haired woman teased.

Wynn grinned at her, pausing to say hello to the stooped little man talking to Mrs. Baker. "Well, can I help it that it's spring?" she laughed. "This is no day to be stuck inside slaving over a typewriter. You won't tell on me, will you?'' she added in a conspiratorial whisper.

The older woman pursed her lips. ''You do a story about my boy Henry and I'll keep your guilty secret,'' she promised.

''What did Henry do?''

''He caught a fifteen-pound bass this morning over at James Lewis' pond,'' Mrs. Baker said proudly.

''You tell him to bring it by my office about two o'clock today and I'll get a picture of it for the paper,'' Wynn agreed. ''Now, how about a soda? I'm parched!''

''What was it this time?'' Mr. Sanders asked with a smile, leaning heavily on his cane. ''A fire? A wreck?''

''Water,'' Wynn corrected, pausing long enough to take the icy soft drink from Mrs. Baker and toss down a swallow before she continued. ''John Darrow had the soil-conservation people help him design and build a pond on his farm to store water in case of drought.''

''Mr. Ed says the early rain means we probably will have a drought this summer,'' Mr. Sanders agreed, quoting his next-door neighbor, a farmer of eighty-two whose claim to fame was that he was more accurate than any south Georgia weatherman.

Wynn took another long sip from the soft drink before she replied, ''I hope he's wrong.'' She grinned at the wrinkled old man. ''Now, *there's* a story. I think I'll go take his picture and get him to predict the rest of the summer.''

''He'd love that,'' Mrs. Baker said, and her blue eyes looked young for a minute. ''He's got grandkids in Atlanta. He could send them all a copy.''

''I'll put it down for first thing tomorrow.'' With a sigh, Wynn sank down beside the wooden fruit bin into a comfortably sway-backed cane-bottom straight chair. ''Just think. I could be sitting in a normal office working a lazy eight-hour day, and nobody would ever call me at night to ask how much a subscription was or how to get a picture in the paper.''

''And you'd hate it,'' the older woman

laughed. She lifted her face to the ceiling fan with a sigh. "Funny how these fans are just coming back into style. This one's been here since I was a young woman."

"I remember sitting here on lazy Fridays in the summer with Granddaddy, just after the fish truck came up from Pensacola," Wynn recalled. "Granddaddy would buy oysters and cook them on a wood stove while my grandmother fussed and swore that I'd burn myself up trying to help him. Those were good days."

Mrs. Baker leaned on the counter. "How's Katy Maude?" she asked.

"Aunt Katy Maude is up in the north Georgia mountains visiting her sister Cattie." The young woman grinned. "She lives near Helen, that little alpine village that looks like Bavaria, and the two of them have been threatening to ride an inner tube down the Chattahoochee this summer."

Mrs. Baker burst out laughing. "Yes, and I'll just bet Katy would do it on a dare! Say, when are you and Andy getting married? We heard Miss Robins say it might be this summer."

Wynn sighed. "We think we'll wait until September, and take a week off for a honeymoon." She smiled, trying to picture being married to Andrew Slone. They had a comfortable, very serene relationship. He made no demands on her physically, and they spent most of their time watching television together or going out to eat. She could imagine their marriage being much the same. Andy wasn't exciting, but at least he wouldn't be rushing off to cover wars like McCabe....

"Will McCabe come back to give you away?" Mrs. Baker asked, as if she had looked into Wynn's mind and picked out the thought.

Hearing his name was enough to cause volcanic sensations in Wynn. McCabe Foxe wasn't her guardian in any real sense. He only held the administrative keys to her father's legacy, doling out her allowance and taking care of her investments until she was either twenty-five or married. At her next birthday, she'd be twenty-four. But before then, she'd be married to Andy, and McCabe would fade away into the past where he belonged. Thank God, she added silently.

"I don't think so," she replied finally, smiling at Mrs. Baker. "He's down in Central America right now, covering that last skirmish for the wire services. And getting fodder for his next adventure novel, no doubt," she added with a trace of bitterness.

"Isn't that something?" the elderly woman sighed, her eyes suddenly dreamy. "Imagine, a famous author whose father was born here," she said. "And he lived just a couple of houses away from you for all those years. Right up until he went into wire-service reporting with your father."

Thinking about that made Wynn uncomfortable. She didn't like the memories of those days.

"Your dad was a good writer," Mr. Sanders interrupted. "I remember those reports of his that Edward printed in your paper, with his byline."

Wynn smiled. "I still miss him. I don't know what I'd have done if Katy Maude hadn't taken me in when he was killed. I've never felt so lost.''

"Good thing your father let McCabe handle the money,'' Mrs. Sanders remarked. "Your mother left quite an estate, and you were still in your teens when your dad died. Only thing is, I do wonder why McCabe let you stay here.''

"He could hardly have taken me with him,'' Wynn pointed out. She finished the rest of her soft drink and placed the empty bottle on the counter. "Well, I'd better get back to the salt mines, I reckon. It's press day and if I know Edward, he'll be calling all over the county any minute to find out where I'm hiding. Nobody escapes when we're putting the paper to bed.''

"I've got to go, too,'' Mr. Sanders sighed, standing up as Wynn did. "Mrs. Jones worries if I don't march in and out on the hour. Amazing how I managed to crawl through trenches all over France by myself in the war without Mrs. Jones behind me to push,'' he added with a twinkle in his eye.

"You just be grateful you've got a house-keeper to look after you who doesn't charge an arm and a leg," Mrs. Baker chided, pointing an accusing finger his way.

"Reckon you're right, Verdie," he sighed.

Wynn laughed at his hunted expression. "Aunt Katy Maude tends to worry about me, too," she admitted. "That's why I moved into the guest house when I got old enough. We get along just fine as long as we don't live together."

"It isn't right for a young girl to live by herself," Mrs. Baker began, "not with that huge house and only Katy Maude in it."

Wynn glanced quickly at her watch. "Oops, got to run," she interrupted with an apologetic smile before the older woman had time to get started on her pet subject. "See you later." She tossed a quarter onto the counter and made a run for the door, laughing, her skirts flying and her pale green eyes shimmering with humor.

But the humor faded once Wynn had started the small car and was roaring away toward

Redvale down country roads that seemed to go forever without a sign of another car or a house. This section of south Georgia was primarily agricultural, and it stretched out like Texas, the land flat or slightly rolling, with only a few farmhouses and country stores to break the rustic monotony.

Thinking about McCabe had upset her. It was ridiculous that it should, that she should let it. He was world-famous now, rich enough to retire and give up risking his life. But he kept on reporting, as if it was a habit he couldn't break, and Wynn had stopped watching the newscasts because she couldn't bear to see what was happening in Central America. She couldn't bear the thought that McCabe might be badly hurt.

It shouldn't have mattered, of course. They had never gotten along and their last confrontation had been sizzling. McCabe had hit the ceiling when Wynn announced that she was joining the staff of the Redvale *Courier*. It had been a telephone conversation, one of McCabe's rare ones, and he'd threatened, among other things, to cut off her allowance. She'd told him to go ahead and do it, she'd support herself. The conversation had gone from bad to worse, and ended with Wynn slamming the phone down and refusing to answer when it rang again. A week later, there was a terse note from him, with a New York postmark, agreeing that a job with a weekly newspaper might not be too dangerous. But he warned her against covering hard news, and threatened to come back and jerk her out of the office if she tried it. "I have my spies, Wynn," he'd written. "So don't think you'll put anything over on me."

She leaned back hard against the seat, her foot easing down on the accelerator. Arrogant, hardheaded man—she still couldn't believe that her father had legally had McCabe appointed executor of his will and Wynn's estate. They were friends, they had been for years. But it seemed ridiculous somehow, when Katy Maude would have been the logical person to put in charge, since she'd had responsibility for Wynn since her childhood, while Jesse Ascot was off covering news.

Where was McCabe now? she wondered. There'd been a report a couple of days before about two reporters being killed in Central America. Wynn had sweated blood when she overheard a conversation about it. She'd butted in, asking if the men had heard who the reporters were. French, they'd replied. French. And she'd gone home and cried with relief. Ridiculous! She was engaged, her life was planned, and McCabe had never been anything to her but a big blond headache.

She drove by Katy Maude's house on the way back to the office. Her eyes caught sight of a curtain fluttering in the guest house where she lived, and she wondered absently if she'd left a window open. Well, it wasn't likely to rain again, so what did it matter?

When she got back to the Redvale *Courier*'s office, nestled between Patterson's Mercantile and the Jericho Drug Company, Kelly Davis was rushing out the door.

"Hi," Wynn greeted the tall, thin young man. "Remember me? My name is Wynn Ascot and I work here."

"Really? You could have fooled me," Kelly replied dryly. "I never see you, and neither does Edward, which means I get stuck with the really gruesome stories."

"Like what?" she asked innocently.

"Like the wreck out on the federal highway," he replied quietly. "One fatality, three injuries. The state patrol just got there."

"Any names yet?" she asked.

He shook his head. "Hope it's nobody we know," he said with a faint smile, and she knew what he meant. This was the really bad part of working for a small-town paper. Two out of three times, you knew the victims, and many of them were friends or family.

"Let us know as soon as you find out, will you?" she asked.

"I'll call before I come back," he promised.

She watched him run for his old pickup truck, and prayed, not for the first time, that it would start. It did, with an ear-splitting roar, and she watched it jerk down the wide street that ran around the tree-lined square with its Confederation statue and old men in overalls sitting on park benches in the shade.

Edward Keene looked up when she came in. He was standing beside the young brunette typesetter at the computer, his heavy white brows drawn into a scowl over his weather-beaten face. His nose seemed to quiver as he clutched the galley proof in his hand. "I'll wait to paste this up until you get that correction line, Judy," he told the typesetter, aiming a glare at Wynn.

"Who are you?" he asked his girl reporter. "Do you work here? Do you know what day it is? Do you realize that I'm making this paper up alone and trying to help Judy proof copy and set ads..."

"I got photos," she said, holding up the camera with a grin. "Big ones, they'll fill up space."

"Pix of what?" he grumbled. "A pond?"

"And a house fire and that new bypass bridge they just finished in Union City."

He beamed. "Really?"

"Well," she sighed, "at least that cheered you up for a minute. Kelly will get the wreck, so that gives you at least four pix for the front page, and we could blow them up to four columns each…?''

''That's why I hired you.'' He nodded with a grin. ''You know how to spread news out. Okay, with what I've already got, that'll fill 'er up.''

''I'll take it back to Jess in the darkroom,'' she said, and started into the other office.

''Uh, after you do that, come into my office for a minute, will you?'' Edward hesitated.

Wynn glanced at him, puzzled. He looked strange for an instant. She shrugged and rushed to the back with the film. It was press day, she told herself. Everybody looked strange then.

She handed the film to Jess with a grin at the harassed look that immediately appeared on his thin, aging face. ''Yesterday?'' he muttered.

''Please,'' she said, agreeing on the delivery date. ''All you have to do is three halftones, though, four columns each—one of the fire and one of the new bridge and one of the pond.''

"I get to pick them out?" he asked with raised eyebrows.

"Sure! See how good I am to you?" she asked as she headed toward the door.

"Good! Here I am with three rush jobs, one to get out by two o'clock, I haven't made the first negative..." He kept right on muttering, and she dashed back into the newspaper office and closed the door.

Edward was sitting behind the heavily loaded desk, which contained a much-used manual typewriter, half a dozen daily newspapers from which he pirated leads, and some scratch paper. He pulled off his glasses and whipped out a spotless white handkerchief to clean them with.

"Well, sit down," he said impatiently, leaning back with his hands crossed over his ample stomach.

"What is it?" she asked, getting scared. He looked...really strange.

"Feel okay?" he asked.

"Sure." She eyed him warily. "Why? Do I look like a potential stroke victim?"

He cleared his throat. "No."

"It's Katy Maude!" she burst out.

"No," he said quickly. His shoulders lifted and fell. "Why don't you keep up on what's happening in Central America? Then you'd know and I wouldn't have to stumble all over myself."

Her blood actually ran cold. She gripped the arms of the chair hard enough to numb her fingers. "McCabe," she gasped. "Something's happened to McCabe!"

"He's alive," he said. "Not badly injured at all."

She leaned back with a sigh, feeling herself grow weak. All these years, she'd expected it, until today, and she'd been knocked sideways. "What was it? A sniper?"

"Something like that." He tossed an issue of the Atlanta morning daily over to her. "Notice the sidebar."

She looked away from the banner headline to the accompanying story. "*WAR CORRESPONDENT INJURED.*" There was a small, very dark photo of McCabe and she strained her eyes to see if he'd changed much over the long years, but she couldn't even make out his features. She read the copy. It stated that McCabe had been hurt while covering a story, and there was some speculation as to whether the incident was connected to the deaths of the two French correspondents that had been reported earlier that week. According to the story, McCabe had been roughed up and had a torn ligament in one leg and a trace of concussion, but he was alive.

"It doesn't say where he is now," she murmured.

"Uh, I was afraid you'd wonder about that. Be kind of hard to miss him, of course," he mumbled.

She stared at him. Her mind was only beginning to work again after its shock. "Hard to miss him?"

"Yes. When you walk in your front door, that is," Edward volunteered. "Big man..."

"He's at my house?" she burst out. "What's he doing at my house!"

"Recuperating," he assured her. "Well, the

motel's closed down for remodeling. Where else could he stay?"

"With you!"

"Nope," he replied calmly. "No spare room."

"He could sleep on the couch!"

"In his condition? Couldn't ask an injured man to do that," he said.

"I could," she replied coldly. "I can't have McCabe in the house alone with me. Katy Maude's not due home for several more weeks, she's just getting over her heart attack, and she couldn't take the excitement of constant arguing."

"You and Katy don't argue," he observed.

"But McCabe and I do," she reminded him. "Constantly. On every subject. And Andy will go through the ceiling!"

"Oh, him," Edward said, dismissing the other man with a wave of his hand. "Andy's one of those liberal city fellows. He won't think a thing about it."

"Are we talking about the same Andrew Slone?" she asked. "My fiancé, who went on local television to protest a theater advertisement in the Ashton *Daily Bugle* because it showed a woman's bare bosom?''

Edward looked at her over his glasses. ''Hmm. You might have a problem there, sure enough.''

''You set me up,'' she accused. ''You invited McCabe here.''

''Well, he suggested it,'' he admitted. ''Called to ask if we'd seen the story in the paper, mentioned what bad shape he was in...I knew you wouldn't mind,'' he added with a grin. ''After all, he's your guardian.''

''Guardian! My tormentor, my inquisitor, my worst enemy, and you've put him under my own roof!'' she wailed. ''Why didn't you send him to Katy Maude's house?''

''Because there's no one in it,'' Edward said reasonably. ''He can hardly walk at all, Wynn,'' he reminded her. ''How would he get along?''

''He's a reporter,'' she ground out. ''He's lived on pure nerve for so long that he'd probably survive without water on the desert!

Doesn't his mother live in New York now? Why didn't he go stay with her?''

"She left the country when she found out he was coming back from Central America," Edward laughed. "You know Marie, she's scared to death to let him get a foothold in her house. He'd have the servants fired and the house remodeled in two days' time."

"Not my house, he wouldn't," she muttered. "Marie always did find excuses to hide out from his father and from him."

"He's hurt," he reminded her. "Poor wounded soldier, and you'd turn him out in the cold!"

Her full lips pouted at him. "You don't know McCabe like I do," she argued.

"He wants to meet your fiancé," he continued. "He's concerned about your future."

"He wants to dictate it, that's why," she growled, standing. "Well, he won't get away with it. He's not going to wrap me around his thumb!"

"Where are you going?" he called.

"Off to war," she called back. "Where's my elephant gun?"

"But the paper—"

"I'll read it later," she grumbled.

"Our paper," he thundered. "The one we won't get out if you don't get in here and help me make it up!"

"I'm taking my lunch hour late," she told him. "I'll be back in an hour."

Edward threw up his hands. "An hour. We're already an hour behind schedule and she'll only be gone an hour. Judy, I tell you..."

But Wynn wasn't listening. She was running for her car, with sparks flying from her green eyes. If McCabe thought he'd been through a war, he hadn't seen anything yet!

Chapter Two

Wynn could sense McCabe watching her even as she opened the unlocked door of the white frame cottage behind Katy Maude's monstrous Victorian house on Patterson Street. She stormed in, her hair flying, her step sounding unusually loud on the bare wood floors and area rugs.

"McCabe!" she yelled, tossing her camera, purse and sweater onto the chair in the hall. But only an echo greeted her.

She turned to go into the living room, which she'd redecorated the year before with western furniture and Indian rugs. She stopped short just inside the doorway and caught her breath.

McCabe was sitting quietly in her big armchair by the fireplace, one big foot propped on the hassock, wearing leather boots and a safari suit that would have looked comical on any native of Redvale. But it suited his dark tan, his faintly tousled thick blond hair, which needed trimming badly.

All the years rolled away. He looked just as Wynn remembered him, big and bronzed and blond—larger than life. His craggy face looked battle-worn, and the light eyes that were neither gray nor blue but a mixture of the two narrowed as they roamed boldly over her slender body.

She stared helplessly, trying to reconcile her memories with the man before her. He seemed to find her equally fascinating, if the searching, stunned expression on his usually impassive face was anything to go by.

"You're older," she said in a tone that was unconsciously soft.

He nodded. "So are you, honey."

Casual endearments were as much a part of him as his square-tipped fingers, but the word caused an odd sensation in Wynn. She didn't understand why, and she didn't like it.

"What are you doing here?" she asked reasonably.

He raised both eyebrows as he lifted the smoking cigarette in his hand to his chiseled mouth. "My plane was hijacked," he said with a straight face.

She pursed her lips. "Try again."

"You don't believe me?"

"Very few planes are hijacked to south Georgia, in my experience," she murmured. The words were just something to keep her mind occupied while her eyes helplessly roamed over him and she tried to fire up the old antagonism.

"What experience?" he asked carelessly, narrowing his eyes as he studied her. "How old are you now?"

"Just months away from my inheritance," she reminded him with a smile. "When Andy and I marry, I'm a free woman."

"Andrew Slone," he muttered, leaning back in the chair with a sigh. "How in hell did you get landed with him? Is he blackmailing you?"

She gasped. "I love him!"

"Elephants fly," he scoffed. He ground out the cigarette in the ashtray on the table beside his chair. "You'd stagnate married to a man with his hang-ups."

"What do you know about his hang-ups?" she challenged.

He met her eyes squarely and a wild little tremor went through her stomach. "Enough to know I'm going to stop you from making the mistake of your young life. I grew up with Andrew, for God's sake, he's a year older than I am!"

"I like older men," she shot back. "And he's just thirty-six, hardly a candidate for a nursing home!"

She stopped herself abruptly. Why should she justify her feelings for Andy to McCabe, for heaven's sake? "What do you think you are, McCabe, the Spanish Inquisition? You don't have any right to burst in here and start grilling me...and what are you doing here, anyway?''

"Don't get hysterical," he said soothingly. "I'm here to help you sort yourself out, that's all. Just until I recuperate."

"I don't need help, and why do you have to recuperate here?"

"Because my mother left the country, servants and all, when she realized I was on my way back," he said nonchalantly. "I let the lease on my apartment expire and the only quarters I have at the moment are in Central America." His eyebrows arched. "You wouldn't want me to go back there to heal?"

She averted her eyes before he could read the very real fear in them. "Don't be absurd," she said.

"Then 'here' was the only place left."

"You could stay at Katy Maude's," she offered. "She has plenty of bedrooms—"

"All upstairs," he reminded Wynn. "And before you think of it, the love seat she had the last time I came home was two feet shorter than I am. You do remember that I'm six-foot-three?''

How could she forget, when he towered over everybody? ''Ed's sofa is plenty long,'' she grumbled.

''His brother-in-law is visiting him next week.''

She moved closer to the chair, her arms folded across her chest, her eyes narrowing suspiciously. ''Odd that he didn't mention that when he told me you were here.''

''It's press day,'' he observed. ''He's out of his mind. Probably cursing you already. Surely you can't be spared right now?''

''I'm on my lunch hour,'' she began.

''Great. I'm starved. How about a sandwich or two?''

''Now, just a minute, McCabe,'' she said forcibly. ''We haven't decided where you're staying yet, much less—''

''I didn't have any breakfast,'' he sighed, laying a big hand on his flat stomach. ''Hardly any supper last night. The press hounded me to death at the airport—'' he peeked up to see how she was reacting "—and I was too tired to go out."

She felt herself weakening and cursed her own soft heart. "Well, there's some ham in the fridge, and I bought potato chips yesterday."

"Ham's fine," he agreed quickly. "Thick, mind, and with lots of mustard. Got some coffee?"

She threw up her hands. "I can't argue with you!"

"You never could, and win," he reminded her. He moved and winced, and his face went oddly pale.

She looked at the big leg resting on the hassock. Ed had said something about a torn ligament, but the shape of a thick bandage was outlined against one powerful thigh under the khaki fabric. A bandage.

Her eyes went slowly back up to his. "That's no torn ligament," she said hesitantly.

His shaggy head leaned back. "Hard to fool another journalist, isn't it, Wynn? You're right. I didn't pull a ligament. You know how the press can make mistakes."

Her own face paled. "You've been shot."

He nodded. "Bingo."

She could feel her heart going wild, her knees threatening to buckle. It was an odd way to react. She drew in a slow breath.

"You *were* with those journalists who were killed, weren't you, McCabe?" she asked with quiet certainty.

His darkening eyes fell to his leg. "I'd just left them, in fact," he said. "We were going to follow an informer to a meeting with a high-level government official. Very hush-hush. It blew up in our faces. I got away by the skin of my teeth and spent the night in a chicken house. I nearly bled to death before I was able to get back to town."

Her heart was hurting now. No one had known what a close call he'd had. It was just dawning on her that he could have died. She felt oddly sick.

"How far did you walk?"

"A few miles. The bullets did some heavy damage, but I was flown to New York and treated by a very apt orthopedic surgeon. I'll have a limp, but at least I didn't lose the leg."

She stared at him, memorizing every hard line of his face. It had been a compulsion, even years ago, to look at him. She enjoyed that even when she imagined she hated him. It was a effort to drag her eyes away.

"I'd better get lunch," she said numbly.

"I'm all right, Wynn," he said quietly, watching her, "if you're concerned with the state of my health. There were times when I imagined you might not mind if I caught a bullet," he added calculatingly.

She avoided his eyes. "I don't want you to die. I never did."

She walked into the kitchen and made the sandwiches automatically, wondering at her own horrified reaction to his wounds. He was in a dangerous business, she'd always known that, and why should it matter? But it did! Her eyes closed and she leaned heavily against the counter. Life without McCabe would be colorless. She had to know that he was somewhere in the world, alive.

With an effort, she loaded a tray with coffee and chips and the sandwiches and carried it back into the living room. McCabe was still sitting where she'd let him; his face was drawn, a little paler than before.

"You're in pain," she said suddenly.

He laughed mirthlessly. "Honey, I've hardly been out of it for the past week, and that's God's own truth."

"Do you have anything to take?"

"Aspirin," he said with a grin. "You know I don't like drugs, Wynn."

"You might make an exception in cases like this," she burst out, sitting across from him on the sofa.

"I'm a tough old bird. My hide's just about bullet-proof."

She handed him the plate with his sandwiches and chips. "How long will it take for it to heal?"

"Another month or so," he said with obvious distaste. "The bone has to knit back properly."

She stared at his leg again. "Are you wearing a cast?"

"No. The bone's not broken clean through.

But it aches all the time, and I don't walk well. There's a lot of me for that bone to support.''

Her eyes ran up and down him quickly. ''Yes, there is,'' she agreed.

''I really do need a place to stay,'' he said over his coffee. ''It's not easy for me to get around in this condition. Surely even in this little town, people will be able to understand that. I don't care about gossip, but I imagine you do.''

''Yes,'' she agreed, glancing at him warily. ''Andy's going to go right through the ceiling, regardless.''

''Let me handle Andy,'' he said generously. ''Man to man, you know.''

That didn't quite ring true, but perhaps she'd misjudged McCabe. She hoped so.

''Won't you be bored to death staying in Redvale for a whole month?'' she asked as she finished her sandwich and washed it down with coffee.

''If I didn't have anything to do, I might,'' he agreed. ''I don't have another book due for six months, and I was between assignments, so I took a job here in town.''

She stared at him with dawning horror. "What job?"

"Didn't Ed tell you?" he asked pleasantly. "I'm going to edit the paper for the next month while he goes on vacation."

Chapter Three

Wynn felt as if she'd been kicked in the stomach. She simply stared at him.

"Edit the paper?" she echoed. "Ed's paper? My paper? You'll be my boss?"

"You got it," he said pleasantly.

"I quit."

"Now, Wynn..."

"Don't you 'now Wynn' me!" she said, setting down her coffee cup with a loud crack. "I can't live with you and work with you for a solid month and stay sane!"

He lit a cigarette and watched her with an odd, quiet smile. "What's the matter, honey, afraid you won't be able to resist seducing me?''

She went scarlet and started to jump to her feet. Unfortunately, in the process, her knee hit the tray and knocked it off onto the floor. Bits of ham and bread floated in a puddle of coffee at McCabe's feet while he threw back his head and laughed uproariously.

Her slender hands clenched at her hips and she counted to ten twice.

Before she could think up something bad enough, insulting enough, to say to him, the phone rang. Gritting her teeth, she grabbed up the receiver.

''Hello!'' she said shortly.

There was a hesitation and a cough. ''Uh, Wynona?''

''Andy!'' she gasped, glaring at McCabe. Her hand twisted the cord nervously. ''Oh, hi, Andy, how are you?''

''Ed said you'd gone home for lunch,'' her fiancé said suspiciously. ''He said you had a visitor. A guest,'' he emphasized. ''Wynona, have you gone crazy? McCabe may be your guardian, and an older man, but he's a bachelor and we're not married and you simply can't let him stay there!''

His thin voice had gotten higher and wilder by the second, until he was all but shouting.

"Now, Andy," she said soothingly, trying to ignore McCabe's smug grin, "you know how it is. McCabe's been injured and he's not even able to walk!''

"Then how is he going to get to bed? Are you going to carry him back and forth!''

She started laughing. She couldn't help it. First McCabe appeared out of the blue with bullet wounds, and now Andy was hysterical....

"Wynona?" Andy murmured.

"Have you got a wheelbarrow I could borrow?" she asked through tears.

"A what? Oh, I see." He chuckled politely, and then sighed. "I'm jumping to conclusions, of course. But I remember McCabe. Can I help feeling threatened?''

"I'm engaged to you," she reminded him, furious at McCabe's open eavesdropping.

"Yes, I know," Andy said, softening audibly. "It just hit me sideways, that's all."

"McCabe is my guardian," she said, glaring at McCabe, who was watching her with a wicked smile. She looked away quickly. "Anyway, he's old."

"He's a year younger than I am," Andy murmured.

"I didn't mean that!" Wynn twisted the telephone cord viciously. "It's press day, Andy, I'm just not thinking straight."

"It's just another Tuesday," her fiancé said shortly. "I don't know why you make such a big thing about Tuesdays."

"You'd have to be a reporter to understand, I guess," she said generously. "Look…"

"Invite him to supper," McCabe said sotto voce.

She gaped at him. "It's Tuesday!" she burst out.

"I heard you the first time!" Andy shouted.

"I'll cook," McCabe said simultaneously.

"Don't be absurd, you can't even stand up!" she threw back at him.

"Are you implying that I'm drunk?" Andy asked, aghast.

"Not you—McCabe, McCabe!" Wynn ground out.

"McCabe's drinking, and you're there alone with him?" Andy gasped.

Wynn held out the receiver and cocked her head at it threateningly.

"Don't do it," McCabe advised. "I can manage to get something together before you come home. I'll sit down and cook."

She eyed him warily. The old McCabe was arrogant and commanding, not pleasant and cooperative, and she was immediately suspicious. "You wouldn't mind?"

"No," he said. "I'd love to see Andy again. Invite him over. About six."

She felt as if she were walking obligingly into a shark's mouth, but it had been years since she and McCabe had spent any time together. Perhaps his experiences had changed him. Mellowed him. She was even in a forgiving mood. Didn't he seem different?

"Andy, come to supper at six," she said, holding the receiver to her ear.

"Supper?" Andy brightened. "Just the two of us?"

"McCabe's here, too," she observed.

"We'll just ignore him," Andy said. There was a pause. "He isn't going to stay for the wedding, to give you away?"

"If he does, we'll let him be bridesmaid," Wynn said darkly.

Andy giggled. "That's cute, McCabe in ruffled satin..."

She started laughing and had to say a quick good-bye and hang up before she really got hysterical.

"Bridesmaid?" McCabe murmured with pursed lips. "Remember that old saying, Wynn—I don't get mad, I get even?"

"I can outrun you," she reminded him.

"Yes. But I'm patient," he returned. His eyes narrowed and ran over her slender body in a way that made her frankly nervous. "I can wait."

"I've got to get back to work. After supper," she continued, moving toward the kitchen to get a towel to mop up the spill, "we'll discuss your new lodgings."

"Suits me," he said obligingly.

That really worried her. McCabe never obliged anybody.

She went back to work with a frown between her wide-spaced green eyes. It deepened when she saw Ed.

"You didn't mention that you were taking a vacation," she said with grinning ferocity. "Or that your brother-in-law was coming to stay in your house. Or that—"

"Have a heart, could you say no to McCabe?" he groaned.

"Yes! I've spent the past seven years doing just that!"

"He's like a son to me," he said, looking hunted as he paused in the act of pasting up the last page of the paper, the front page, with a strip of waxed copy in one hand and a pair of scissors in the other. "He's been shot to pieces, Wynn."

She straightened wearily and the fight left her. "Yes, he told me."

"I just hope he'll give himself time enough to heal completely before he goes back down there."

She felt the blood leaving her face. "You can't mean he's talking about going back?"

He shrugged. "You know McCabe. He loves it, danger and all. It's been his life for too many years."

"He could stay home and write books!" she threw back. "He's a best-selling author, why does he need to risk his life for stories someone else could get?"

"Ask him." He cut off another column of copy and pasted it around another story in neat pieces, just right for a two-column headline. "I think it's the lack of an anchor, Wynn. He doesn't have anyplace that he feels wanted or needed, except at work."

"His mother loves him."

"Of course she does, but she's spent her life avoiding his father...and now, McCabe. She's independent, she doesn't need him. And who else is there?" he added.

She stared blankly at the half-made-up page. "At his age, there must be a woman or two."

"No."

She looked up. "How do you know so much about him?"

"I helped raise him, remember? He used to hang around my house as much as he stayed at his own. We've kept in touch all this time." He glanced at her over his glasses and smiled. "I always wanted to be a war correspondent, you know. But I had a family, and I didn't feel I had the right to take the risk. McCabe's shied away from permanent relationships for much the same reason, I imagine. Rough thing for a woman to take, having her man on the firing line most of their married lives."

Wynn had thought of that, but she wasn't admitting it. Neither was she admitting how many newscasts she'd chewed her fingernails over before she stopped watching them altogether, or the kind of worrying she'd done about McCabe over the years. He shouldn't matter, of course, he was only her guardian.

"Wynn, are you listening?" Ed asked shortly. "I said, I've still got a hole on the front page. Go call the fire chief and see if they've had any fires overnight, okay?"

"Sure thing, Ed."

The hectic pace kept her from thinking about McCabe any more until quitting time. The phones rang off the hook, people walked in and out, there were additions and deletions and changes in ads and copy until Wynn swore she'd walk out the door and never come back. She threatened that every Tuesday. So did Ed. So did Judy. So did Kelly and Jess. It was a standing joke, but nobody laughed at it on Tuesday.

At five o'clock, the pages were pasted up and Kelly was driving them the thirty miles to the printer. The wreck Kelly had covered earlier took up a fourth of the front page. It had been a tragic one involving people from out of town, two carloads of them. Wynn was sad but involuntarily relieved that no one from Redvale had fallen victim. It was harder to do obituaries when you knew the victims.

She dragged herself in the door at a few minutes past five, weary and disheveled and feeling as if her feet were about to fall off from all the standing she'd done. She already missed the air-conditioning at the office. She didn't have it at home, and it was unseasonably hot.

"Is that you, Wynn?" McCabe called from the kitchen.

"It's me." She'd forgotten for an instant that he was here, and her heart jumped at the sound of his deep voice. She tossed aside her purse and paused to take off her suede boots before she padded in her hose onto the tiled kitchen floor.

He glanced up from the counter where he was perched on a stool, making a chef's salad.

"Long day?" he asked, glancing down at her feet.

"You ought to know," she returned. "Can I help?"

"Make a dressing, if you don't have a prepared one."

"What's the main course?" she asked, digging out mayonnaise and catsup and pickles.

"Beef bourguignon. Do you like it?"

She stared at him. "You didn't mention that you did gourmet dishes."

"You didn't ask." He turned on the stool to study her. His shirt was open down the front, and she kept her eyes carefully averted. McCabe, stripped, was a devastating sight. She'd seen him that way at the pool, of course, wearing brief trunks that left his massive body all but bare. He was exquisitely male. All bronzed flesh and hard muscle with curling thick hair over most of it. Wynn didn't like seeing him without a shirt. It disturbed her. Seeing Andy the same way didn't, and that disturbed her, too.

"You look bothered, honey," McCabe commented, flicking open another button, almost as if he *knew!*

She cleared her throat. "I need to change first, before I start this," she said, leaving everything sitting on the counter while she escaped to her bedroom.

She closed the door and slumped back against it heavily. What was wrong with her, anyway? McCabe was the enemy. Unbuttoning his shirt wasn't going to change that, for heaven's sake! Was she an impressionable girl or a woman? She shouldered away from the door. A woman, of course!

Ten minutes later, she went back into the kitchen and McCabe stopped with a spoon in midair above the stew and just stared.

The dress was emerald-green jersey. It had spaghetti straps that tied around her neck and across her back, leaving it bare to the waist behind. It outlined her high breasts, her small waistline and the deep curve of her hips with loving detail, and clung softly to her long legs when she walked. With her long hair piled atop her head and little curls of it hanging around her neck and temples, she was a sight to draw men's eyes.

"Do you wear dresses like that often?" McCabe asked, scowling.

"Of course I do," she said softly, and turned away. "Are you through with supper? I'll finish making the dressing."

"Not in that dress you won't," he said curtly. He moved, leaning heavily on his stick, and was behind her before she knew it. One big warm hand caught her waist firmly and held her away from the counter. "It would be a crime to ruin it."

Her body tingled wildly under his hard fingers, as if she'd waited all her life for him to touch it and bring it to life. She felt herself tremble and hoped he wouldn't feel it.

"You...shouldn't be standing," she reminded him.

"You sound breathless," he murmured, and she felt his warm breath in her hair, like a heavy sigh. His fingers moved experimentally to her hip and back up again, as if they were savoring the feel of her. She wanted to lean back against him and let them inch up, slowly....

She gasped and moved jerkily away from him. "I...I'll get an apron," she faltered. "Andy will probably be here any minute, he's almost always early!"

McCabe didn't say a word. He stood quietly by the counter, leaning against it and the cane, and watched her with darkening eyes that didn't leave her for a second.

She glanced at him nervously as she fumbled with jars and bowls and spoons. "Say something, will you?" she laughed.

"What is there to say?" he asked softly.

She tried to speak, tried to find words to diffuse the tension between them, but instead she looked into his eyes and ached all the way down to her toes.

Before she could move, or run, the doorbell rang sharply and saved her the effort.

She turned and walked like a zombie to the front door and opened it.

Andy's brown hair was rumpled, as if he'd been running his hands through it angrily, and his dark eyes were troubled. He stared down at Wynn, but didn't really seem to see her at all.

"Hi," he murmured. "Supper ready? I'm starved."

She sighed and led him back toward the dining room. "Come and say hello to McCabe first," she said.

Andy made an irritated sound. "Does he really cook?"

"Of course I do, Andy," McCabe said from

the kitchen doorway, leaning heavily on his cane. He'd done up his shirt and looked presentable again, the picture of the courteous host. Like a lion bleating, Wynn thought wickedly.

"Good to see you again, Andy," he said. He extended his left hand, the right one being busy with the cane.

Andy automatically put his own hand out, but reluctantly. "Hi, McCabe," he said coolly. His eyes ran up and down the bigger man. "Got shot, I hear."

McCabe's eyebrows went up. "Did you? I thought it was a torn ligament in the paper."

Andy flushed and glared at Wynn. "You said…"

"No, I didn't," she said curtly. "Did you call Ed? You did, didn't you? You couldn't take my word—?"

"Now, children," McCabe said smoothly, "suppose we dispense with the squabbling until after supper? Heated-over beef bourguignon is so tacky, don't you think?"

Andy gaped at him. "Beef bourguignon?"

"In my humble way, I enjoy gourmet cooking," the bigger man said with disgusting modesty, almost blushing. Wynn was ready to choke him. McCabe, sounding like a society leech...

But Andy was falling for it headfirst. He laughed easily and grinned at Wynn. She could read the thoughts in his mind, the sarcasm. Big-time war correspondent. Adventure novelist. He-man. And he makes beef bourguignon and uses words like "tacky."

"Sit down and I'll bring it in," McCabe told them.

But Wynn was horrified at the thought. "You sit down," she said coolly, glaring at him. "I don't want stew all over my floors. How in the world do you expect to manage a tureen of that plus your cane?" She went into the kitchen, still muttering.

By the time she had everything organized and started carrying in the filled coffeepot and service, the heated rolls and beef bourguignon and salad, there was an odd silence in the dining room. McCabe was leaning back, smoking a cigarette, and Andy was looking...

"What's wrong, Andy?" Wynn asked quickly.

He glanced at her and blushed. "Uh, nothing. Can I help?"

"No, I've only to bring the dressing." She shot a glare at McCabe as she went to fetch it.

Supper was a quiet affair. She nibbled at her beef bourguignon—which was truly excellent, wine red and thick and full of melty bits of beef and vegetables and salad—and wondered why Andy was so quiet.

"We had a bad wreck today," she mentioned, trying to break the cold silence. "Some out-of-state people—"

"For heaven's sake, not while I'm eating!" Andy burst out, making a face at her.

McCabe's eyebrows went up sharply. "Are you still squeamish, Andy?" he asked politely. "Yes, I seem to remember that you never enjoyed our biology class coming just before lunch." He leaned back with his coffee in hand and pursed his lips. "The formaldehyde was nauseating, wasn't it? And those dissections..."

Andy had turned green and was putting down his spoon. He grabbed his ice water and drank and drank.

"Stop that, you animal," Wynn growled at McCabe. "How could you?"

"I like science," he replied imperturbably, watching Andy. "Did I ever tell you about the food I had in South America when I was covering the conflict down there a few years back? I went deep into the Amazon with some soldiers and we camped with a primitive tribe in the jungle. We had snake and lizard and some kind of toasted bugs—'

"Excuse me," Andy gasped, leaping to his feet with a napkin held tightly over his mouth. He ran toward the bathroom and slammed the door.

"McCabe!" Wynn burst out, banging the table with her hand.

He sipped his coffee. "If he can't stand to hear about your work, what will you talk about when you're married?" he asked politely. "Or do you plan to stick to conversation about textiles from now on?"

"You don't understand—"

"I understand very well." He held her eyes and frowned.

"What's wrong?"

He leaned forward and turned her face toward his. "You've got a smudge, just here." His big warm hand pressed against her cheek while his thumb ran roughly back and forth across her lips.

It was the most sensuous thing she'd ever experienced in her life, more sensuous than Andy's most ardent kiss. Her lips parted helplessly as she looked into his darkening eyes, and his thumb crushed her upper lip and then her lower one. She felt her eyes narrowing helplessly, her breath coming wild and fast, her mouth parting, trembling, at the blatant seduction of his touch.

"Like it?" he breathed huskily, watching her mouth.

She caught his hand and started to pull it away, but he brought her palm up to his mouth and caressed it softly, tenderly, while his eyes held hers.

Oh, don't, she pleaded silently. But she was going under, and her eyes went helplessly to his mouth and she wanted it with a shocking hunger.

"Come on," he whispered, tantalizing her. "Come on, Wynn."

She was actually leaning toward him across the scant inches that separated them when the sudden sharp click of the bathroom door opening sent her jerking back into her own chair.

Andy came back into the room looking pale and furious. He sat back down in his chair and took a long sip of his ice water.

"Feeling better?" McCabe asked pleasantly.

Andy glowered at him. "No thanks to you."

"Reporters do bring the job home, Andy," the taller man commented. "It's pretty hard not to, in this business. You'll find that there are going to be times when Wynn will need to tell you about things she's seen, to save her sanity."

Andy looked at him uncomprehendingly.

"Wynn and I understand each other very well, thanks," he said curtly. "She knows I'll listen if she needs to talk."

"Of course I do," Wynn began placatingly, stilling her trembling hands in her lap.

Andy turned to speak to her and his eyes went homing to her swollen mouth, devoid of lipstick and looking as if it had been hotly and thoroughly kissed. His face flamed and he drew in a harsh breath.

Wynn put a hand to her mouth, as if she could cover up what McCabe's thumb had done to it. "Andy, it wasn't what you're thinking," she said shortly.

"Sure it wasn't." Andy stood up, almost knocking over his chair. "He's only been here a day, for heaven's sake!"

"I'm a fast worker," McCabe said with a wicked smile. "And Wynn is a dish. Can you blame me? Especially when she's so... responsive."

Andy seemed to puff up. His face reddened and he gave Wynn a killing glance. He whirled and slammed out of the house. A minute later, the roar of his car filled the silence.

"You troublemaker," Wynn accused hotly. "What was the point of that lie?"

"It wasn't a lie," he said calmly, lighting a cigarette. His eyes shot up and held hers. "You'd have let me kiss you."

She shifted restlessly. "All right," she admitted, "I probably would have. We go back a long way and I'm as curious about you as you seem to be about me. But I'm engaged to Andy, I'm wearing his ring. And what's a kiss, these days, McCabe?"

"It depends on the people involved," he said quietly. His eyes scanned her hot face. "You and I would make more of it than a meeting of mouths."

She flushed and dropped her eyes to her empty coffee cup. "He'll pout for three days before he even speaks to me again. That is, if he doesn't break the engagement."

"You'd be better off."

"I don't want to be an old maid," she burst out, glaring at him. "It may suit Katy Maude, but it wouldn't suit me. I don't like being alone, living alone!"

"You aren't," he reminded her. "You're living with me right now."

"Not in the sense I mean."

"Not yet," he agreed, and it was a threat.

She stood up. "I'll do the dishes."

"Running?" he asked, studying her. "I won't go away. And neither will the problem."

"I'll ignore you both," she promised him. She gathered the dirty dishes, but as she started by him, to add his plate to the pile at the end of the table, he caught her around the waist and turned her, pressing his open mouth to her backbone.

She stiffened at the unexpected contact. His big hand spread out across her midriff, bringing her closer as his lips brushed between her shoulder blades down to her waist. His hand moved slowly, insidiously, to the flatness of her stomach and back up in a warm, lazy circle. Her hand went to catch it, to stop it, and lingered helplessly on the curling hair that covered the back of it.

He let her go all at once and she moved

away from him as if she'd been scalded, with wild eyes that glanced off his.

"You really are a babe in the woods," he murmured, watching her hands tremble as they stacked dishes. "Hasn't Andy ever done that to you?"

She lifted the stack, praying she wouldn't drop it. "Wouldn't you like to know?" she asked coldly.

"Wynn..."

She paused at the doorway to the kitchen, with her back to him. "Yes?"

"Imagine how it would be," he said quietly, "if I kissed you all over like that."

The dishes tottered precariously in her hands and she marched into the kitchen stiff-legged, viciously kicking the swinging door closed behind her.

She took her time doing the dishes, tingling all over with the force of her own awakened hungers. McCabe should be shot, she told herself. Then she remembered that he *had* been, and felt guilty.

She finished washing up and went reluctantly back into the living room. She had to get this situation in hand, she had to convince McCabe that she wouldn't tolerate any more of his suggestive remarks. She was engaged, she belonged to another man. Besides, what would McCabe want with her? A little fling between assignments? A pleasant diversion while he recuperated? Because he wasn't a marrying man—he'd told her that himself years ago. And Wynn couldn't settle for an affair. She wanted a marriage, a husband, children. Which made it doubly irritating that McCabe could make her feel sensations Andy's wildest ardor had never aroused. And by barely touching her.

Sorting words and explanations in her mind, she marched into the living room ready to do battle. And found McCabe sitting up asleep in his easy chair.

In sleep he was oddly vulnerable. The hard lines in his broad face were relaxed, his lips were slightly parted. His eyes were closed, heavy-lidded and copper-lashed, under the deep jutting brow. His hair wasn't a true

blond, it was a pale brown with blond high-
lights, bleached by sunlight. There were dark
hairs in his eyebrows, too, and in the opening
of his shirt she could see dark and light min-
gling, his curling hair like a shadow under the
khaki shirt. He was as broad as she remembered him, his chest tapering down to a flat
stomach and narrow hips. The muscles in his
legs bunched sensuously under the fabric of
his trousers. She tingled all over, just looking
at him. She always had. But it had made her
angry when she was a girl, and it made her
angry now, that he should cause such a reaction in her. He was the enemy. Wasn't he?

"Deep thoughts, Wynn?" he asked lazily,
and his eyes opened to slits.

"You weren't asleep at all," she accused,
embarrassed at being caught in that total scrutiny.

"No, I was resting my eyes. If my leg didn't
hurt so much, I'd let you sit on my lap," he
added with an outrageous grin.

The thought of it made her feel odd. She
turned away. "McCabe, we've got to talk."

"All right. Sit down. Better yet, make some coffee and then sit down."

"I already have," she murmured, glad of a reason to escape. "I'll bring it in."

She calmed down while she got the coffee service, and when she'd poured the black liquid into cups and was sipping hers, she was able to face him quite calmly. Outwardly, at least.

"How do you like it?" he asked suddenly.

She blinked. "Like what?"

"Reporting."

"Oh." She smiled. "I love it. It's not at all like a normal job. It's exciting and there's variety, and I feel like I might even be doing a little good once in a while."

He nodded. "And you learn a lot. About life, and people, and professions. It's an educational kind of job. An information clearing house."

"The press releases we get are really interesting," she agreed eagerly. "We can't begin to print them all, we don't have the space, but I love reading them just the same. We get inside features on racing and medicine and all sorts of political profiles, scientific discoveries…it's almost as good as working in a library.''

"And you learn how government works," he murmured dryly.

"I wouldn't be a politician for all the opals in Australia," she burst out. "Oh, McCabe, isn't it terrible? So much controversy over even the smallest decisions, and if you tell the truth you cause all kinds of trouble for everybody. But you can't *not* tell the truth, because you're obligated to."

"It goes with the job." He grinned. "If you do it right, both sides hate you."

"So I've found out." She sighed. "And no matter how hard we try, we make mistakes. And while nobody remembers the good jobs we do, nobody forgets the bad ones."

"The wreck bothered you, didn't it?" he asked after a minute, studying her over the rim of his coffee cup. "Why?"

She shrugged. "There was a child involved. Two years old. He was killed."

"Who else?"

"The baby's father." She looked up at him. "The baby's mother is in a coma. If she lives, think what a horrible awakening she's going to have. I wouldn't want to live, I don't think." She laughed mirthlessly. "And do you know why it happened? The driver of the second car was in a hurry to get to Atlanta. He had an appointment." Tears welled in her eyes. "He didn't want to be late, so two people died."

He sighed heavily. "Wynn, you can't judge. Especially, you can't afford the luxury of getting involved. It's suicide."

"Stop caring, you mean?" she asked. "Stop hurting when I see someone else hurting?"

He shook his head. "I mean you have to learn to report the news without becoming part of it. Death is a natural part of life, honey. I've seen more of it than I care to remember in the past few years; lives wasted in ways you haven't dreamed of. But you can't cry for every death. You'd never stop. You have to change your perspective."

"How?"

"You simply learn to take it one day at a time," he said, and his eyes darkened. "You have to understand that people are going to die. You can't stop it. You can't help by walking around in a perpetual state of grief. You have to report what you see and go on. And if you can't handle what you see, it's time to quit."

Her eyes ran over his craggy face. "Can you still handle it, even after what you've seen?"

He smiled carelessly. "Barely."

"Why?"

"Why do I do it?" He shrugged. "Somebody's got to. I'd hate to see a family man step into my shoes. Nobody would miss me—"

"Don't," she ground out, averting her eyes. "That's a horrible attitude."

There was a long silence and she felt his gaze almost physically.

"Wynn, don't brood over me," he said after a minute. "I can take care of myself. Heaven knows, I'm not suicidal."

She glanced up. "Sure you can. Look what good shape you came home in!"

He chuckled softly. "So I slipped up. Everybody's entitled to one mistake."

"It was almost your last."

"That, too." He leaned back with a heavy sigh. "Does Andy ever listen when you talk shop?"

She flushed and avoided his penetrating gaze. "I don't ask him to."

"He doesn't," he said, answering his own question. "So who do you talk to? Ed's like me, he doesn't look back. Who's left?"

"I talk to myself, if you must know," she muttered. "I'm a sparkling conversationalist when I get started."

His eyes narrowed. "And that's exactly why I wanted you out of this business. You're not tough enough, Wynn. One day you'll fold up like an accordion."

"That hasn't happened yet," she reminded him. "And I'm tough, too, like my father was."

He smiled softly. "I owed your father my

life once or twice,'' he recalled. ''He pulled me out of some hairy situations. I'm only sorry I couldn't do the same for him, the one time it mattered.''

''He admired you,'' she said.

''It was mutual. That's why I agreed to this crazy scheme of his, to oversee your inheritance.'' His eyes wandered over her slowly. ''But I'm just beginning to understand his reasoning.''

''If that's another dig at Andy, you can forget it,'' she told him, rising. ''He's well-to-do, he doesn't need my money.''

''He doesn't need your money,'' he mused, ''he doesn't want your body, and he doesn't seem to need common interests either. What exactly do you do together?''

Her jaw fell. ''We get along very well,'' she tossed back. ''We go to movies, we like the same kind of books, we're good friends...''

''You're describing a brother, not a potential lover,'' he shot back. ''Do you want him?''

''That's none of your—''

"Because you *do* want me," he continued, watching her flush. "And I want you."

Her breath sighed out wildly and she fought to retain control of the situation; her hands clenched at her sides until they whitened. "McCabe..."

His head went back and he studied her arrogantly, intently. "It's just as well I stayed away so long, Wynn."

She hardly understood what he was saying. She was too embarrassed. "It's been a long day. You can have the spare bedroom. It's—"

"The first one down the hall," he said for her. "I scouted around when I got here."

"Naturally." She picked up the coffee service and carried it back to the kitchen, not bothering to wash up the two cups. "There are towels and washcloths in the bathroom if you want a bath," she told him. "I take mine early in the mornings."

He stood up with an effort, his face lined with pain. "I could use a good soak," he agreed. "One way or another, it's been a long week."

"When do you start at the office, since Ed never tells me anything?" she asked.

"In the morning." He smiled at her irritation. "I can ride in with you, if you don't mind."

"I don't, but *you* might," she murmured, sizing him up. "I drive a Volkswagen."

"I'll bend over double, it will be all right," he assured her. "'Night, Wynn."

"Good night, McCabe."

He watched her go down the hall with a purely predatory gaze. And slowly, calculatingly, he smiled.

Chapter Four

Wynn hardly slept. All night, she kept feeling the touch of McCabe's hard mouth on her back until her skin felt unbearably sensitive. Images of him whirled through her head and shocked her. When morning came, she was feeling dragged-out and irritable.

She dressed in faded denim jeans and a T-shirt with "Foxy Lady" emblazoned across the front, because it was Wednesday and they'd all be working in the back to mail out papers. It was dirty work, because newsprint came off on hands and clothes and skin as the hundreds of papers were bundled and bagged and sent to the post office. Everybody wore casual clothes on Wednesday.

She ran a brush through her long hair and left off her makeup. It didn't matter. Her complexion was an artist's dream, peaches and cream, and her bee-stung mouth hardly needed the gloss of lipstick she gave it.

McCabe was already dressed and in the kitchen, trying to make toast. He was wearing brown slacks and a patterned shirt, open at the throat, with a lightweight tan jacket and tie. He turned as she walked in and chuckled at the expression on her face.

"I wear jeans in the jungle, honey," he murmured, approving of hers, "but the first day on the job I don't want to scare off the help."

"You won't do that," she said. He looked so good, Judy would probably swoon. Wynn honestly felt like it herself, so she dragged her eyes away.

"Here, I'll do that. Why don't you sit down?"

"I'll be sitting all day," he sighed angrily. "Dammit, I hate inactivity!"

"You won't get much of that, handling Ed's job," she murmured, smiling at him as she made the toast and poured coffee. "Want some eggs or bacon?"

He shook his head. "Can't stomach it this early. How about you?"

"The same, I'm afraid." She handed him his coffee and sat down by him.

"Andy called."

She lifted her head. He looked odd. "When?"

"About six."

She glanced at her watch. "Over an hour ago? You didn't wake me."

"I asked Andy if he wanted me to hand you the phone," he murmured.

It took a minute for that to sink in. Her eyes scanned his face and she began to flush. "You didn't!" She got to her feet in one smooth motion. "McCabe, you didn't!"

"I did." He sipped his coffee calmly and raised an eyebrow at her. "He is suspicious, isn't he? He jumped immediately to the conclusion that you were in bed with me."

She lifted her saucer and slammed it down on the table, shattering it into a dozen pieces. "That's it, that's it, you're leaving here today! I don't care if you have to shack up with a mouse, you are leaving my house! How dare you interfere in my life? I'll marry whom I please!"

He got to his feet with the help of the cane and moved toward her. "Not Andy," he said quietly.

"Yes, Andy!" She backed away from him. "You just pack your bags, McCabe Foxe, and I'll drive you to a motel."

"No, you won't," he said. "I'm not leaving."

"I'll call the police," she threatened wildly as she wound up with her back to the wall and McCabe looming over her.

"How interesting," he said. "What will you tell them?"

She thought about that for a minute. Infuriatingly, she couldn't think of anything.

"No go, Wynn," he said with a laugh. "You're stuck with me, so make the most of it. It won't be so bad."

"But it is bad," she wailed, staring up at him with a wildly beating heart, intimidated by the sheer size of him. "Oh, McCabe, you're going to ruin my whole life."

He shook his head. "No. I'm going to help you salvage the rest of it. Andy isn't for you. He'd drain the life out of you."

"But it's my life," she returned.

He looked down into her wide green eyes and lifted his hand to brush her hair away from her face in an oddly tender gesture. "I won't let him have you."

"You don't have that choice, McCabe!" she burst out. "You can't tell me what to do, I'm not sixteen anymore!"

"I never told you what to do," he reminded her. His hand brushed down her throat and across her collarbone while he held her eyes and studied them. His fingers brushed lower, across the top row of letters on the T-shirt, over the soft tops of her breasts, and she gasped, and knocked them away.

"You'll let me do that one day," he said quietly. "In fact, Wynn, you'll lift the blouse out of my way yourself."

She ducked under his arm and moved away from him on shaking legs. "You should live so long," she shot at him.

But he only smiled.

They got to the office at eight-thirty, and McCabe went immediately into Ed's office and sat down behind the big desk.

"Get the staff in here," he said without preamble.

"Kelly's still in school," Wynn reminded him.

"Then get Judy and Jess in here."

"Yes, sir, Mr. Editor," she said smartly, and went to fetch them.

When they piled into the office, McCabe was frowning over a copy of the last week's edition. He looked up and waited patiently for Wynn to introduce him. He acknowledged the other staff and grinned.

"Don't believe a word Wynn tells you about me, it's all lies," he told them. "I'm laid up for a while, so Ed thought this would be a great time to go on vacation and dump the paper in my lap."

Wynn glared at him, but he ignored her.

"I don't plan to start any exposés or turn this into the world's greatest crusading weekly over the next month, in case the thought crossed anyone's mind," he added. "You do your jobs and I'll try to do Ed's and we'll all lie when he gets back and say it was impossible without him. Okay?"

Jess and Judy laughed and went back to work. McCabe grinned at Wynn. "Well, don't you have anything to do? Or—" he motioned her closer and whispered in her ear "—would you like to close the door and we'll make love on the desk?"

She glared at him. "Please stop mistaking me for one of the vulgar heroines in your vulgar books," she said coldly, and moved toward the door.

"I didn't know you read my books," he murmured, watching her blush. He grinned. "Remember which page that particular scene was on, do you, Wynn?"

She felt herself go hot all over. She did remember it, vividly, because when she'd read it she could almost see McCabe bending over the Latin girl in the book.

"Oh!" she burst out.

He lifted his shaggy head and smiled wickedly. "It's a very interesting way to do it, on a desk."

She went out and slammed the door behind her.

"Something wrong?" Judy asked, lifting her brows.

"I quit," Wynn said shortly.

Judy shook her head. "Wrong day. This is Wednesday. You threaten to quit every Tuesday, remember?"

Jess went after the papers just before noon, and by the time Kelly got to the office, Wynn was knee-deep in them. Jess stamped the papers that went out to local post offices, while Wynn put the single-wraps that went outside the local area into prestamped lightweight brown bags. McCabe handled the phone and the front office while the rest of them sacked and lifted and tied bundles and loaded the truck that carried the papers the five miles to the post office. By the end of the day Wynn was black down the front from newsprint and her face was smeared with it. She was more than ready to go home and have a nice hot bath.

She was just about to leave the office when Judy motioned her to the telephone.

"Hello," she said dully.

"Wynn?" Andy asked, his tone conciliatory. "Would you like to have dinner with me tonight?"

She brightened. "I'd love to. And despite what McCabe might have told you, I sleep alone," she added curtly.

"He just rattled me, that's all," came the embarrassed reply. "I can't keep my wits around him."

You're not the only one, she thought, but didn't say it. "What time are you coming by?" she asked instead.

"Around six. We'll drive up to Columbus and take in a play, too."

"Sounds great. I'd better rush home and dress," she added, glancing at her watch.

"How wonderful that the presses didn't break down. That's what usually happens when I've got someplace I have to be on Wednesday afternoon." She grinned. "See you later."

She hung up and went back into the office to get her purse. "If you're riding home with me," she told McCabe without looking at him, "I've got to go. Andy's taking me to Columbus."

He didn't reply, and she turned, purse in hand, to find him sitting stiffly in the chair with a face like chalk. One big hand was resting on his thigh and he was as taut as a drawn rope.

"McCabe!" she cried softly. She put the purse down and went closer. There were beads of sweat on his brow. He looked terrible.

"Could you find me an aspirin, honey?" he asked curtly. "Or, failing that, a saw?" he added dryly.

"Here." She dug out a powerful over-the-counter painkiller that she kept for Katy Maude's arthritis attacks. "Two of these will work better than aspirin——if the publicity on them is reliable."

She got him a soft drink from the machine in back and opened it for him, watching him swallow down the pills.

"I keep forgetting what condition you're in," she sighed, sitting back down at her own desk. Her worried eyes scanned the drawn lines in his face. "Can I do anything?"

"Get me the saw," he ground out. He rested his shaggy head against the high-backed swivel chair and closed his eyes. "God, I hurt, Wynn."

"You might have stayed home today, where you belong," she chided.

"I can't run a newspaper from the bedroom," he returned. "I couldn't let Ed down."

"He'd have understood. He could have waited."

"I couldn't," he said oddly, glancing toward her. "It's worse when I can't move around."

"Suppose I run you by Dr. Taylor's office," she suggested softly. "And just let him prescribe something?"

His eyes darkened. "I don't like drugs."

"Will you be reasonable?" She glared at him irritably. "McCabe, this isn't an everyday thing, and it isn't permanent, but how are you going to get well if you're drawn up with pain all the time?"

"I'll compromise. Get me a bottle of Scotch and I'll numb it with that."

She pursed her lips. "Soaking it in alcohol is supposed to help?" she asked with a wry smile.

He scowled. "I meant I'd drink it."

"Alcohol," she reminded him, "is a drug."

"Dammit!" he burst out.

"Don't jerk around like that, you'll make it worse." She studied his leg. "McCabe, have you changed that bandage since you left New York?"

He looked uncomfortable. "It doesn't need changing every day."

"When was the last time?"

"Well..."

"When?"

He glared at her. "Oh, three or four days, what difference does it make?"

"It could get infected, you crazy man," she almost yelled at him.

"Well, it's awkward and hard to get to," he grumbled.

"I'll do it for you," she said.

He lifted an eyebrow and studied her. "You do realize that you can't do it through my trousers?"

The blush started at her cheeks and worked its way up. "While you're at Dr. Taylor's—"

"I'm not going to Dr. Taylor's."

She drew in a very deep breath. "Then you'll have to take care of it yourself, you stubborn man," she added.

She wore neat white slacks with a thin white lacy top for her date with Andy and she piled her hair coolly on top of her head. McCabe had settled downstairs with a legal pad, making notes, and he looked comfortable propped up on the sofa in his slacks and shirt. The sleeves were rolled up, the neck was open, and he looked faintly dangerous. Wynn was glad she wasn't going to be subjected to all that masculinity tonight. She felt drunk on him already, and he'd only been back two days. It was explosive to have him under her roof, especially with the innuendos and approaches he'd been making.

She checked her handbag to make sure she had her key, and glanced at McCabe.

"Will you be all right alone?" she asked.

He laughed softly. "If you could see how I've lived for the past six years, you wouldn't ask."

"I guess you've gotten pretty good at taking care of yourself," she admitted.

"I've had to." He studied her for a long moment. "How did you wind up with Andy?"

She turned her small purse idly in her hands. "We'd always known each other, of course. His sister Marilee is my best friend. Then I did a story on their father's textile company, and we started dating. One day he handed me a ring and I put it on." She shrugged. "I suppose it sort of just happened. We get along well, we have common interests…"

"But you don't want him," he said quietly.

His eyes searched hers. "If you marry him, feeling that way, you'll be cheating him, Wynn."

"There are more important things," she began.

He shook his head. "Equally important things," he corrected, holding her gaze. "Come here."

She hesitated, but when he held out a big hand she went forward like a puppet to give him her own.

His fingers inched between hers and tugged gently until she sat down on the sofa beside him, so that his broad chest was pressing warmly against her thigh.

His free hand let go of the legal pad, letting it fall to the floor, and he slowly unbuttoned his shirt while his darkening eyes held hers. He drew her fingers down and brushed them against the feathery hair on his broad chest.

"McCabe..." she began uneasily, and tried to draw her hand back.

He pressed it, palm down, against him. "Do you ever touch Andy like this?" he asked quietly.

"No," she admitted. "If it's any of your business, I don't. May I have my hand back?"

"Why don't you?"

She stared at him. "Well, because…" She sighed with exasperation. "Because I've never wanted to, that's why!"

"Has he touched you that way?"

She felt her cheeks burn as she met that knowing gaze. "Look, it's getting late, and Andy will be here any minute and I'm not ready!"

"You are, except for your shoes." He studied her upswept hair critically. "If you were going out with me, I'd make you take down your hair. I don't like it screwed up like that."

"You don't have to like it." The feel of his body under her hands was wildly disturbing, and keeping him from knowing that was becoming impossible.

His eyes wandered down to her thin blouse and began to darken. "You aren't wearing a bra under that. Why?" he asked coldly.

She felt her cheeks blaze. "McCabe Foxe!" she burst out, dragging her hand from his.

"Does Andy like it that way?" he demanded, watching her jerk to her feet and glare at him. "Does it make it easier for him to stroke your—"

"Stop it!" she burst out, horrified. She folded her arms across her breasts.

"Put something on under that top before you leave here, or, by God, I'll do it for you," he threatened, sitting up. "You're not going out with him, looking like that."

"I'm a grown woman, I can wear what I like," she began hotly.

He swung his legs gingerly off the sofa and started to get up. She ran wildly for the bedroom, locking the door behind her with a slam. She cursed and paced and mumbled for ten minutes. But she put on a bra.

McCabe was lying back on the sofa again when she reentered the room, still scribbling on his legal pad. He glanced up, giving her breasts a brief but thorough scrutiny.

"That's better," he said curtly. "There's no sense in tempting a man beyond his limits."

"Andy and I are engaged, for heaven's sake!" she reminded him.

He looked up into her eyes with a quiet, intent gaze. "An engagement doesn't make a marriage. I want to be the first, Wynn."

It took a minute for that to sink in, but when it did she blushed all the way to her toes. His words robbed her of speech as she stood there with incredulity in every line of her face.

"I will be, too," he continued softly. "So I think you'd better give Andy back the ring."

"Of all the horribly conceited men," she began, glaring down at him, "to think you can come walking back into my life out of the clear blue and start taking it over."

He smiled slowly, mockingly. "But that's exactly what I'm going to do, honey. And you're going to let me. Before I leave Redvale again, you're going to belong to me from your green eyes down to your toes. All of you. In ways you've never dreamed of belonging to a man."

"You just keep right on hoping, McCabe," she said icily. "I love Andy."

"Sure you do. Like a brother." His head lifted and he smiled slowly. "But you want me, Wynn."

Chapter Five

"You're quiet tonight," Andy commented as they sat in a Columbus restaurant eating prime ribs and a green salad.

Wynn looked up guiltily. "Am I? Sorry, it's been a long day."

"It's McCabe, isn't it?" he muttered, glaring at her. "He looked like black thunder and you were barely speaking to him when I came to get you."

"If you must know, we had a disagreement," she lied.

Andy sighed. "Well, why don't you just ask him to leave?" he burst out, falling for it.

"He won't go."

"I'll see about that," Andy told her, and straightened proudly.

Even with a bum leg, McCabe would have made mincemeat of him, and she knew it. She laid a hand over his. "He won't be here long, Andy."

"One day is long enough for him to make trouble. He's after you," he said, his eyes concerned.

She knew that, but she wasn't admitting it. "He's my guardian. My legal guardian, just that."

"You're so innocent, Wynn," he groaned. "You don't know the arsenal a man like McCabe would have, you'd be no match at all."

She looked away before he could see the expression in her eyes or the blush that threatened to tell him everything that had happened earlier.

"I don't know what to do," he sighed, watching her. "I feel like an outsider since McCabe came back."

"He's wounded, Andy," she reminded him.

"Yes, that's true enough." He brightened slightly. "But you must know how it looks, having him in the same house with you all the time. People are going to start talking eventually."

"People who know me won't think anything at all," she said shortly.

"Won't they?" he replied. "I'm thinking things, Wynn."

She glared at him. "How could you? You know perfectly well—"

"He said he'd hand you the phone!" he accused hotly.

She flushed wildly. "He was lying! Andy, can't you see that he's trying to break us up? And you're helping him by jumping to wild conclusions!"

He still looked ruffled, but he seemed to calm a little as he sipped his coffee. "I don't like him. He's too cocky."

She almost laughed. Arrogant, yes, but cocky? It didn't fit McCabe at all. She finished her dessert and sipped her black coffee. "Anyway," she said, "he'll be gone as soon as his leg heals."

"It won't be soon enough to suit me," he grumbled.

That was exactly how Wynn felt about it, but she kept her thoughts to herself. She didn't want Andy to know just how vulnerable she felt with McCabe. She changed the subject, and they went to see a comedy at a local theater before they drove back to Redvale, apparently in perfect accord for the time being.

It lasted to her front door. Andy walked her to the porch, and was just giving her his usual gentle good-night kiss when the door opened and McCabe appeared, staring at them with icy disapproval.

"What do you mean, bringing Wynn back home at this hour?" McCabe asked curtly, checking his watch. "Do you realize it's almost one in the morning? What will people think?"

Andy was flabbergasted. He stared and stumbled. "We're...we're engaged..." he managed.

"What has that got to do with anything?" McCabe demanded. "You keep her out this late again, Andy, and you'll regret it."

And before Andy could decide what to say, McCabe had jerked Wynn into the room and slammed the door.

"Where were you?" he asked curtly.

She stared at him with her mouth open. "Eating supper," she stammered. "And seeing a play."

"And what else?"

"Nothing else!" She tossed down her purse and glared at him, getting some of her wind back. "What business is it of yours how late I stay out? And how dare you give my fiancé the third degree!"

"My, how your eyes do sparkle when you get mad," he murmured approvingly.

"Stop that," she muttered. "Besides, to interrupt us like that—"

"Missing your good-night kiss, honey?" He chuckled, moving closer. "Come here, and I'll take care of it for Andy. It's the least I can do."

"Don't you dare!" she exclaimed as he reached for her. She pushed at his broad chest, but he only tugged her closer. She aimed a kick at his leg, but he sidestepped, getting his long, undamaged leg between both of hers in a hold that was disturbingly intimate.

"Trying to kick an injured man," he laughed. "Shame on you."

"Let go of me, then," she panted, struggling.

"Not yet," he murmured, bending her down over the broad back of the sofa, so that her torso was laid against it helplessly. "Ah," he whispered, lowering his head, "I always wanted to try it like this."

Before she could ask what he meant, he was showing her. His mouth opened slightly before he slid it against her lips, and his eyes stayed open the whole time, watching her.

"McCabe!" she burst out, feeling trapped and shocked and just a little apprehensive.

"Don't start having the vapors," he breathed against her lips. "I just want to kiss you."

"You mustn't…not like this," she whispered.

His hands moved hers over her head as his chest eased down over hers, and he chuckled at the gasp that escaped her. "Mmm, isn't this erotic?" he whispered. "Making love on the back of a sofa."

"Stop!" she burst out.

"Stop what?" he asked. His cheek moved against hers as his lips smoothed over soft skin, down into the neck of her dress. "You smell of gardenia. Sultry and sweet and womanly." His nose rubbed softly against hers and the feel of him was beginning to do the wildest kinds of things to her pulse. She felt her breasts flattening under the crush of his chest, smelled the tangy scent of cologne and soap, felt the warm abrasive brush of his jaw. Her hands touched his cheeks hesitantly before they moved up into the cool thickness of his blond hair.

"That's it, darling," he whispered. "Now, just relax and let me show you how…."

His mouth coaxed hers open with a tantalizing pressure that made her wild with need long before he satisfied it. She opened her eyes lazily, her mouth following his helplessly, hungrily, her breath coming fast and hard in her throat as she looked up at him.

His eyes smiled down at her just as she felt the hard, hungry crush of his mouth in a tiny consummation that satisfied the spiraling hunger and created an even more monstrous one.

It was the wildest sensation she'd ever felt. Like flying into the sun. She arched up against him, surging with hungers she'd suppressed all her life, until this moment.

He lifted his head to look at her, and all the teasing was gone. "Andy wouldn't dream of something this pagan, would he, Wynn?" he breathed roughly. "He'll kiss you at the door and think you're satisfied. But I won't." His mouth caught hers, a little bruisingly. "I'll wrestle you down on sofas or sand or fur rugs and raise hot desires in you. And then I'll drag you into the inferno with me and watch you burn up." His mouth slid down her throat, onto her soft breasts, and she cried out at the unfamiliar, frightening sensation as the touch penetrated the layers of fabric. It was like skin on skin, and her fingernails dug into the nape of his neck painfully.

He jerked up, his eyes glittering as they met hers, and he smiled slowly when he recognized the hot wildness in her gaze. "You're passionate, Wynn. Andy isn't. And that's what's eating you up. Because I can match you, and he can't."

It was like a dash of cold water. Her eyes lost their eagerness and flashed with anger. She aimed a slap at his face, but he caught her hand and pressed the palm to his mouth.

"Let me up!" she burst out, struggling until she could roll out from under the weight of his chest. She got away and stood glaring at him, her eyes wild, her hair a glorious tangle, her very posture expressing fury.

He straightened, grimacing as he put pressure on his game leg. But then he grinned. "Greenhorn," he accused with a laugh. "You didn't even know how to kiss. And you're supposed to be an engaged woman?"

"Andy respects me," she panted.

"I respect you, too. Take your clothes off and I'll show you how much," he said with a stage leer.

"Shame on you!" she burst out.

"Respect has a different meaning for me," he told her. "I respect you enough to want all of you, not just your mind. A man who could spend several weeks engaged to you without progressing further than kisses is no prize, Wynn. Better you should discover that now than after you're married. You took fire when I kissed your—"

"Stop!" she burst out, preventing the word even as it was forming on his mouth.

"Well, you do get the idea, don't you?" He pulled a cigarette from his pocket and lit it, watching her all the while. "You're sweet to make love to."

"I'm going to bed!" she burst out, defeated.

"Without kissing me good night?"

She almost threw something at him. But she couldn't think of anything big enough to make a dent in his monumental arrogance, so she turned and stormed into her bedroom and slammed the door violently.

The next morning after a miserable night, she put on her most demure everyday dress, a green shirtwaist, with spiked heels, and put up her hair. It gave her confidence, and she was going to need every ounce she had to cope with McCabe.

She walked into the dining room, where McCabe was sitting calmly drinking coffee.

"Good morning," she said quietly. "Did you sleep well? How's your leg?"

"I'll live," he said, watching her. "Are we into disguises this morning?" he added.

She glared at him. "I'm wearing my working clothes."

He laughed softly. "Are you?" He checked his watch. "We'd better get into the office," he said finally, rising. He was wearing gray slacks with a gray-and-white-striped pullover shirt, and he looked male and vibrant.

"Sure," she said, quickly finishing her coffee. "I've got a meeting with the mayor at ten to discuss that new water system he's trying to sell to the city council. Will you want me to drive you to the Rotary Club meeting at noon? Ed always goes.''

"Jess can drop me off on his way to lunch and Kelly can pick me up on his way to the office," he said.

He climbed into the Volkswagen with her, watching her like a hawk all the way to the office.

"Is my makeup smudged or something?" she asked as she parked in front of the *Courier* building.

He shook his head. "I'm trying to puzzle you out, honey," he drawled, and his gray eyes were narrow and intent.

"I wouldn't waste my time, if I were you," she murmured. "After all, you'll be gone before long. Back to what you love most." And she was out of the car before he had time for a reply.

Wynn was out on the streets minutes later. She stopped by city hall to check out a rumor about a drug bust the night before, and found that it was just that. She took a photo of a lushly blooming dogwood tree with two little girls in sundresses under it as a human-interest piece. Then she went to the mayor's hardware store in town to interview him about the water system.

"We're growing fast, you know, Wynn," Harry Lawson told her, a twinkle in his black eyes as he leaned back in his office chair. "We're only using about two hundred thousand gallons of water a day right now, but as we add industry, that figure is going to increase. We have to have a permit to draw water out of the river, and if we don't up our allocation and update our pumping equipment and treatment facilities right now, we may be out in the cold as the water need increases statewide."

"Industry has to have water to operate, and lots of it, doesn't it?" she asked, pen poised over pad.

He nodded. "It depends on the industry. A chicken-processing plant of moderate size would pull around a million gallons a day alone. And a heavy-water-using industry would probably keep our water department in the black for a change.''

"What condition are we in right now?'' Wynn continued.

The mayor sighed. "You've tasted our city water—you tell me. The whole water system is deteriorating. We've let it go for years without any major repairs and now we're paying for it. That's one reason I've asked for emergency funds from the governor's office to take care of the immediate problem. But beyond that, we've got to expand while we can still get the water allocation we need. And that will cost money.''

"Is it really a health hazard, the way it is?''

"Yes, ma'am,'' he said. "And you can print that. Now, here's what we plan to do if we get our emergency money,'' he added, and began to outline the immediate improvements that had to be made.

"What are your long-range goals?''

He grinned. "Well, if we're going to get more water, we have to be able to utilize it.''

"What you're suggesting is that we add another pumping station and additional treatment facilities and expand our water system out into the county," she continued.

"That's right. The more water consumers we bring in, the more revenue we bring in. I don't have to tell you that our water system runs in the red."

"But the taxpayers will ultimately foot the bill for the expansion," she challenged.

"Progress costs," he returned. "If we don't grow, we die. That isn't much of a choice, is it?"

She grinned. "Nope."

When they finished the interview she went out to the city water department and did a photo layout on the existing facility and called the city engineering firm in Ashton to request a drawing of the proposed system. Then she called a few local citizens at random to ask what they thought of the expansion project. It took the rest of the day to do that and write the story. But when she was through, it was enough, with the pictures and drawings, to very nearly cover half of the front page.

"I," she told McCabe at quitting time, "am a genius. I have single-handedly saved you six gray hairs worrying about what to put on the front page by doing a super story on the proposed water system."

"Let's have it."

She handed it to him and watched while he read over her copy and frowned.

"What's wrong?" she asked, nervous.

He glanced up. "The mayor is proposing to finance this with a government grant?"

"Part of it," she agreed. "With another bit to come out of the governor's emergency fund and some assistance from the regional commission."

"That's still going to leave a tidy sum owing," he said.

"He plans to float revenue bonds for that."

He studied her. "You've done your homework," he said with grudging admiration. "What do you know about water usage north of here?"

"I know that Atlanta and surrounding metropolitan counties are going to be pulling almost four hundred million gallons of water per day by the turn of the century,'' she told him. ''I've got a study on it in my desk.''

He grinned slowly. ''Good girl. Okay, we'll do it, with pix, as the lead story, unless something bigger comes along by Tuesday.''

''I told you I was a genius.'' She grinned.

His hand caught in the hair at the nape of her neck. ''You're more than that,'' he breathed, his mouth poised over hers. ''I'll ask you again.... Want to try it on the desk?''

Her mouth parted as she tried to get words out, just as Judy walked in and cleared her throat. ''Uh, Mr. Foxe, telephone,'' she said.

Wynn fought to get herself back together while McCabe talked to a potential advertiser.

''I'll send Wynn over to talk to you, Mack,'' he told whoever was on the other end of the line.

Her poise fell apart. ''But it's quitting time,'' she protested.

''In the morning,'' he added to the customer. ''Sure. Thanks for calling. So long.'' He hung up. ''You ought to know we don't go by banker's hours here,'' he reminded Wynn.

"I'm tired,'' she muttered.

"I'm feeling a little low myself,'' he agreed, studying her. "We'll all call it a day.''

They were no sooner home than the phone rang. McCabe picked it up, listened, glared at it and handed it to Wynn.

"It's Romeo,'' he growled. "Don't tie up the line, if you don't mind. I've got a call coming through from New York.

He hobbled off and she glared at his retreating back.

"Hello?'' Andy mumbled.

"Hello, Andy,'' she said.

"You didn't get into any trouble last night, did you?'' he asked. "I meant to call sooner, but I got tied up.''

"I'm fine,'' she replied.

"Good. McCabe looked...I wish you'd get him out of the house, Wynn.''

"Why don't you come and do it for me?'' she asked with venomous sweetness.

He cleared his throat. "I've got to do some

paperwork," he said. "How about dinner next Friday?"

"Sure."

"See you soon, darling," he said. "Good-bye."

"Good-bye," she mumbled into the phone, wondering all the while how in the world she'd managed to get tangled up with a man like Andy in the first place. Not that she was going to admit that to McCabe.

He glared at her when she joined him in the kitchen, where he was putting mayonnaise on slices of bread.

"My, my, you do have long conversations with your loved one, don't you?" he asked.

Her nostrils flared. "You did ask me to keep it brief. Besides, what I have with Andy is, as I seem to remind you constantly, none of your business."

"Like hell it's not," he said. "You aren't marrying him."

"Would you like to bet on it?" she asked pleasantly.

"Why bet on a sure thing?" he asked,

glancing at her with maddening humor. "Shut up and help me make the sandwiches."

She glowered at him while she layered pastrami and swiss cheese on the bread, along with sliced tomatoes and lettuce. He was close to her, and she could feel the warmth of his body, the heat that radiated from him. It brought back memories of being crushed between his hard chest and the back of the sofa, and she knew that she'd never again be able to look at that piece of furniture without blushing. Perhaps she'd sell it when he left.

Her eyes lifted to his profile. "That phone call you're expecting," she said uneasily. "It wouldn't be from your wire service?"

He glanced down at her, frowning. "Of course."

She lowered her gaze to the sandwiches, cutting them in half with tremendous concentration.

"Wynn, I'm still on the payroll," he said quietly. "I'm taking a leave of absence, that's all."

"Yes, of course," she said, wondering why

it mattered so much that he planned to risk his life again.

He laid down his knife and turned to her, and she could feel his eyes on the top of her head. "I'm a reporter," he said. "A writer. I do a job that I love, and I'm lucky enough to get paid for it."

"You don't have to explain it to me," she said tautly.

He tilted her face up to his. "Don't I?" He searched her face for a long moment. "I like everything up front. I'm here for a rest, and to help you get sorted out. Then I'll go where they send me. Back to Central America, or to the Middle East where that new violence has broken out, or to the Far East...wherever the job calls me. I'd prefer to stay in Central America, but I take the assignments I'm given."

Her eyes searched his. "You write adventure novels, too," she reminded him coolly. "You've made the best-seller list several times."

"And someday I'll write novels for the rest

of my life, and I'll enjoy that, too. But, Wynn,'' he murmured, cupping her face in his hands, ''I'm still a young man. Too young and too restless to settle down. I don't want any ties.''

''I'm young too,'' she reminded him. ''But I want a husband and a family. And Andy is—''

His face closed up, his eyes darkened. ''Andy is a first-class stick in the mud. I want someone better for you.''

''What did you plan on doing, kidnapping someone?'' she asked politely. ''For heaven's sake, I'm a grown woman!''

''Some woman,'' he scoffed, searching her face. ''You didn't even know how to kiss.''

''Thank you for remedying that small fault,'' she said, eyes flashing. ''Now that I know, I'll teach Andy. It should be fascinating!''

His nostrils flared, his hands on her face tightened. ''You can't teach passion to a man,'' he said curtly. ''Either it's there or it isn't.''

"You know so much about it," she flashed. "You and your sexy heroes and your oh-so-eager heroines!"

"Where did you get these archaic notions about sex?" he asked, exasperated. "Not from your father, I'll bet."

"I live in a small town," she reminded him.

"Your aunt, I suppose," he sighed, watching her flush. "Well, honey, I wish you'd keep in mind the fact that Aunt Katy Maude never married and probably thinks sex consists of five minutes of painful groping in the dark."

She blushed to the roots of her hair. "Don't you make fun of my aunt!" she growled.

"Look at you blush," he laughed softly. "Is that what you think sex is, too?"

Her eyes fell to his chiseled mouth and she felt herself go trembly. "No, I don't," she muttered.

She felt his breath on her nose as his face moved down. His hands tilted her chin up, and his eyes held hers.

"If it weren't for Andy, my leg, your morals and a few other irritating obstacles," he breathed, "I'd carry you to bed and love all those repressions right out of your mind, Wynn."

The flush got worse. "Surface relationships are cheap," she ground out.

"Sure they are," he agreed quietly. "But what we'd give each other wouldn't be that, and you know it. If I took you, we'd share something neither of us would ever get over."

That was what she was afraid of, although she couldn't admit it.

"You're supposed to be looking out for my interests," she reminded him shakily.

"Oh, I am," he assured her, bending. "And I'll let you know the minute I find them. Kiss me, Wynn."

She tried to protest, but the minute her lips opened, his found them. It was the night before all over again, the silken webs of sensation taking her into their folds, making her weak and trembly as he drew her body into total contact with his. She felt the hard warmth of him with a sense of awe at his strength, even in his battered condition.

His hands left her face when she didn't struggle, to catch her hips and draw them close against his.

She gasped and tried to pull away, but he held her firmly.

"Don't fight, darling, you'll hurt my leg," he breathed at her lips.

"McCabe, don't hold me...like that," she protested.

"Andy never has, I gather." He kissed her lazily, knocking her protests away while his thumbs did impossible things at the edges of her hipbones, finding their way to her warm, soft belly and making it contract wildly.

She cried out at the rush of sensation and he released her swollen mouth long enough to study her eyes.

"What a waste," he whispered, and his voice sounded husky and deep. "Andy will never satisfy you. Not in a hundred years."

"But you could?" she whispered shakily, trying to force sarcasm into her tone.

"I hope I could," he said softly. His hands moved slowly up to her waist, pressing there.

"You're...so uninhibited, Wynn. All softness and sweet fire. You make me feel weak at the knees."

He did the same thing to her, but she was beyond telling him that. Her eyes looked up into his and she felt his hands moving restlessly at her waist.

"You're tangling me up in a web I don't like," he murmured absently.

"I didn't ask you to come here," she managed.

"Yes, I know. But I needed something," he said. His hands shifted onto her rib cage, and he drew back to watch them against the soft green fabric of her dress. "I didn't even know what, at the time."

"And now you do?" she asked breathlessly as his hands smoothed up and down just above her waist.

"I think I needed to know that it would matter, if I died," he said unexpectedly, lifting his eyes to catch the surprise in hers. "Do you know what Ed told me, Wynn? He said that you wouldn't even watch newscasts about Central America."

She swallowed down a surge of nervous energy. "I don't like international news," she said inadequately.

"Every reporter likes news of any kind," he replied. "It's in the blood. Were you afraid for me, Wynn?"

She dropped her eyes to his chest, seeing the shadow of hair under it, and wondering uncharacteristically what would happen if she opened his shirt and touched him.

"I'd be afraid for anyone over there," she parried.

His hands on her waist contracted. "Just anyone?"

"I've known you for a long time," she muttered, lowering her gaze to his chiseled mouth. "Of course it matters."

"Why don't you go into politics?" he asked. "You're so damned good at avoiding the issue, you'd be a natural."

"I'm not avoiding anything." She pushed at his chest. "Oh, McCabe, stop confusing me!"

"Then stop avoiding the issue," he murmured, bending his head. "Stop throwing Andy between us."

She lifted her head to protest, but before she could get the words out, or he could carry through with what his eyes were threatening, the phone rang again and broke the spell.

He let her go reluctantly and went to answer it, and she made a beeline for her bedroom, leaning back exhausted against the door. McCabe was tearing her safe world apart, and she didn't have the faintest idea how to stop him.

Chapter Six

Eventually Wynn had to come back out, but she went straight to the kitchen to get her sandwiches without glancing at McCabe. She put them on the table and sat down beside him with her coffee.

He looked odd, as if the phone call had disturbed him.

"Something wrong?" she asked with studied carelessness.

"No," he murmured, glancing at her with a frown. "Just the office, checking on me. I told them I was on the mend."

She dropped her eyes to her plate and began

to eat mechanically. His face was lined, as if with pain. "McCabe, are you keeping that bandage changed properly?" she asked.

"Jess did it for me at the office," he said.

She nodded, and he moved the conversation to a safe topic. That night set the pattern for the next week. McCabe kept conversation general, and so did Wynn. She said nothing more about having him move out, having realized just how much pain he was actually in. Sometimes he just sat for hours at a time, as if he dreaded the agony of trying to stand up. She felt her heart go out to him, but only for old times' sake, she told herself. If he wanted to go off and risk getting himself killed, that was his concern.

At least he seemed to have temporarily called a halt to interfering with Wynn's engagement. But she was unsure about his intentions, and he was unpredictable. And since that long, hot kiss she'd exchanged with him, she was understandably nervous.

Andy had accepted her stumbling explanation of McCabe's interference, but he remained stiff when she mentioned the other man's name.

After a hectic week, Andy took Wynn to dinner. McCabe hadn't said anything when Andy came to pick her up, aside from a curt nod and a glare for Wynn.

"Well, at least he's stopped grinning at me like a Cheshire cat," Andy remarked over dinner. "That made me nervous. Maybe he's finally accepting me."

Wynn didn't believe that for a minute, but she held her tongue.

"He isn't making passes at you?" Andy finished.

She grabbed up her coffee and almost spilled it. "No, he isn't," she said with a hard glare, hating both herself and Andy for the lie.

Andy flushed. "Well, don't blow up at me," he exclaimed. "I haven't done anything."

She drew in a steadying breath. It was always like this, with Andy on the defensive while she felt like a heel for snapping at him. Just once, if he'd snapped back...

An image of McCabe flashed into her mind, the way he'd forced her down on the sofa, the way he'd held her and enjoyed feeling her fight him. He had enjoyed it—there was no mistake about that. His eyes had glittered and he'd smiled. She couldn't picture Andy with that hot enjoyment in his eyes, that purely sensual appreciation of her spirit. Andy would be frightened if she attacked him.

"Would you like dessert?" Andy asked after a minute, smiling as if nothing had happened at all.

She sighed. At least he didn't sulk—not often, anyway. That was a blessing. But the making up could have been so sweet, if he'd been like McCabe. She hated herself for that thought, and reached out and squeezed Andy's hand because of it.

"I'm sorry I snapped," she said gently.

"Yes, well, I guess it's something you can't help," he agreed. He squeezed her hand back. "Want to go to a movie?"

She felt ruffled but she smiled and nodded.

They went to see a violent picture that Andy

wanted to watch, a thriller with blood and gore that made her ill. She sat stiffly beside him with her eyes lowered through most of the picture.

"Why do you like that kind of movie?" she asked as they were driving home. "It's terrible. Nothing but savagery and horror."

"I don't know," he said mildly. "It's exciting, I guess. Don't you like excitement? Isn't that why you like being a reporter?" he added deliberately.

"If you mean do I enjoy the gory side of my job, you're out of your mind, Andy," she said hotly. "I don't have a blood lust; frankly, violence makes me ill."

"Then why do it?"

She leaned her head back against the seat and sighed. "You couldn't understand in a million years," she said quietly.

He glanced at her angrily. "You keep telling me that, as if I'm totally stupid. No, I don't understand why a woman would want to subject herself to that kind of work. I used to think it was because you used to have such a crush on McCabe, that you felt you had to follow in his footsteps.''

She blushed angrily. "I never had a crush on him!''

"My sister said you did,'' he persisted, his eyes narrowing. "She said you used to watch him like a hawk and find all sorts of excuses to walk by his house when he was out in the yard.''

To her shame, she had, but she hadn't expected that Marilee, her best friend, would ever rat on her. And to Andy, of all people! Thank goodness, Marilee was married and living in Virginia or heaven knew what she'd make of McCabe staying in the house with Wynn.

"I was just a kid,'' she reminded him.

"You aren't now. And he looks at you... oddly,'' he said, studying her. "Didn't you see the glare he gave me when I put my arm around you? As if you were his personal property! I tell you, Wynn, you've got to get him out of that house. People are starting to talk all over town about it.''

"Andy, you know what kind of condition he's in!" she exclaimed. "You've seen yourself that he can hardly stand up."

"He manages to get to the office every day, though, doesn't he?" Andy asked. "And he hobbles around there very well."

"That doesn't mean he's capable in other areas," she said hotly.

"How do you know?" he asked suspiciously. "Have you tried?"

It was a good thing they were pulling into her driveway, because she'd have jumped out onto the highway rather than put up with another second of his suspicions.

"How can you say such a thing about me?" she burst out.

"Well, you blush every time I mention his name," he muttered, studying her like some new insect. "You get hot and bothered the minute he walks into a room. And there's more than one position for people to make love in."

She blushed at the insinuation and slapped him. Andy just looked horrified.

Get 3 Books FREE!

MIRA BOOKS, the brightest star in women's fiction presents

The Best of the Best™

Superb collector's editions of the very best romance novels by the world's best-known authors!

FREE BOOKS!
Get one free book by **Debbie Macomber**, one by **Linda Lael Miller** and one by **Charlotte Vale Allen!**

FREE GIFT!
Get a stylish picture frame absolutely free!

BEST BOOKS!
"The Best of the Best" brings you the best books by the world's hottest romance authors!

3 FREE BOOKS!

▲ To get your 3 free books, affix this peel-off sticker to the reply card and mail it today!

Get All 3

*W*e'd like to send you three free books to introduce you to "The Best of the Best." Your three books have a combined cover price of $16.48, but they are yours free! We'll even send you a lovely "thank-you" gift—the attractive picture frame shown below. You can't lose!

free!

free!

free!

DARING MOVES
by Linda Lael Miller
"One of the hottest romance authors writing today."
—*Romantic Times*

PROMISE ME FOREVER
by Debbie Macomber
"Debbie Macomber's stories sparkle with love and laughter."
—Bestselling author Jayne Ann Krentz

SOMEBODY'S BABY
by Charlotte Vale
"An excellent read."
—*Ren*

MIRA

© 1996 MIRA BOOK

Books FREE!

DETACH AND MAIL CARD TODAY!

HURRY! Return this card promptly to get 3 FREE Books and a FREE Gift!

The Best of the Best ™

YES, send me the three free "The Best of the Best" novels, as explained on the back. I understand that I am under no obligation to purchase anything further as explained on the back and on the opposite page. **Also send my free picture frame!**

Affix peel-off 3 FREE BOOKS sticker here.

Name

Address

City

State   Zip

183 CIH A2RH (U-BB6-97)

Offer limited to one per household and not valid to current subscribers. All orders subject to approval.

PRINTED IN U.S.A.

The Best of the Best™—Here's How it Works

Accepting free books places you under no obligation to buy anything. You may keep the books and gift and return the shipping statement marked "cancel." If you do not cancel, about a month later we will send you 3 additional novels and bill you just $3.99 each, plus 25¢ delivery per book and applicable sales tax, if any.* That's the complete price, and—compared to cover prices of $5.50 each—quite a bargain! You may cancel at any time, but if you choose to continue, every month we'll send you 3 more books, which you may either purchase at the discount price...or return to us and cancel your subscription.
*Terms and prices subject to change without notice. Sales tax applicable in N.Y.

If offer card is missing write to: The Best of the Best, 3010 Walden Ave., P.O. Box 1867, Buffalo, NY 14240-1867

BUSINESS REPLY MAIL
FIRST-CLASS MAIL   PERMIT NO. 717   BUFFALO NY

POSTAGE WILL BE PAID BY ADDRESSEE

THE BEST OF THE BEST
3010 WALDEN AVE
PO BOX 1867
BUFFALO NY 14240-9952

NO POSTAGE
NECESSARY
IF MAILED
IN THE
UNITED STATES

She swallowed. "I'm sorry you have such a low opinion of me," she said unsteadily.

He rubbed his cheek. "I'm sorry," he said in a strangled tone. "I'm sorry I said that, Wynn, I know you're innocent."

"Do you? How?" she asked coldly.

He cocked his head. "Well, I assumed..."

"As it happens, you're absolutely right about McCabe and me," she said, feeling the words burst out of her in indignation and anguish. "We're lovers. I sleep with him every night. He's wonderful in bed, Andy, really wonderful."

He blanched and his hand lifted. He slapped her with the strength of his arm behind his thin fingers, and she didn't even cry out. Slowly she took the ring from her finger and dropped it on the floorboard. Then she opened the door and got out, leaving him alone in the car.

The house was quiet, although there was a light burning in the room where McCabe slept. Wynn didn't even wonder if he'd gone to sleep with it on. She went to the liquor cabinet where she kept a bottle of bourbon for the rare occasions when Andy brought business acquaintances over for dinner. She poured a generous measure into a glass, added ice and water, and proceeded to get soused.

It had been a cool night, and she was wearing a well-fitting black skirt with a lacy white blouse and bolero jacket. But now it was getting hot, so she took off the jacket and unbuttoned the blouse until her lacy bra showed under it. She took down her hair, too, because it was oddly constricting piled tightly on her head. She kicked off her shoes and stretched out on the couch, feeling more relaxed by the minute.

She was halfway through her second glass when McCabe made an appearance. He was still dressed, although his shirt was out of his pants and hanging open. His thick blond hair was ruffled, as if his hands had worried it, and he was limping badly.

"What are you doing?" he asked, running his eyes over her as she staggered to her feet.

"Getting drunk," she said.

"I can see that. But why?"

She lifted the glass in an exaggerated toast and swallowed the rest of it down quickly. "Ahh," she sighed, closing her eyes briefly with a smile. "How delicious. Isn't liquor great? I wonder why I never drank before?"

He moved closer, his eyes seemingly drawn to the unbuttoned blouse even though he dragged them back to her face. Then he saw the livid red mark on her cheek and his eyes exploded with anger.

"Did he hit you?" he asked coldly.

"Who, Andy?" She laughed and turned to go back to the bottle, but he threw down his cane and jerked her around to face him. Sober, she'd have been frightened of the look on his face.

"I said, did he hit you?"

"Yes, he hit me," she muttered. "And it's all your fault, McCabe. All your fault." She broke his grip only because he let her, and moved away from him to the darkened window. She felt morose and reckless, all at once. "You're my lover, did you know?" she asked with a laugh, turning in time to catch the utter shock on his face. "Andy thinks so. So does everybody else around here, from what he told me."

"That's a lie," he said curtly. "Everyone with any sense knows I'm your guardian. I'm twelve years your senior!"

"Yes, I know, but your old age doesn't fool anyone," she murmured. Her eyes ran over his broad bronzed chest with the thick wedge of hair that ran down it to his belt buckle. "You have the most marvelous body," she said, as the liquor dragged the truth out of her. "And you're good to look at and famous and you write books that only an experienced man could write, so what do you expect people to think? Most of them don't know you think of me as a wet-behind-the-ears grade-school kid."

His eyes darkened even as she spoke and his face hardened. "Wynn, you're drunk."

"I sure am, darling. Isn't that what you called me the other night before you kissed me? I didn't tell Andy you kissed me, Mc-Cabe."

"I'm glad about that, at least," he muttered.

"No, I just told him we were lovers," she continued, and laughed at the shock that widened his eyes. "Well, it was what he wanted to hear. It just confirmed all his evil suspicions."

"What got into you?" he burst out, running an angry hand through his hair. "Don't you realize he's going to repeat it?"

"Let him," she said carelessly. "I even gave him back the ring." She put down the glass and leaned back against the small bar. "Why don't you come to bed with me, McCabe, and I'll let you have your wicked way with me?" That sounded Victorian and amusing, and she laughed.

He was looking wilder by the minute. "You'd better shut up before you say something you'll regret."

"Oh, I'll be like that famous French singer and regret nothing, darling," she said in a mock accent. Her hands went to her blouse and she unbuttoned the last two buttons and unclipped her bra, pulling the whole crumpled

mess down her arms before he could get to
her.

"I'll even take off my clothes..." she was
offering.

He caught her, pushing her roughly back
against the bar while he clipped the bra back
in place, his face oddly strained, his eyes dark
and glittering. He took her arm and pulled her
toward the hall.

"But don't you want my clothes off?" she
asked dizzily.

"Get in there," he said harshly, "and put
on your gown while I make some black coffee.
You're going to hate us both in the morning,
yourself most of all!"

He thrust her into her room, snapped on the
light and hobbled painfully back to get his
cane.

With an uncaring sigh, she stripped off her
clothes, smiling and singing softly to herself,
and dragged on an old cotton gown. She felt
wonderful.

"I'm not engaged anymore," she sang, col-
lapsing on the bed on her back. "Poor Andy,

how will he live without me? He'll have to take total strangers to watch those gory movies with him. Someone who likes blood...do you like blood, McCabe?'' she asked as he returned, his face like thunder. He slammed a cup of black coffee onto her bedside table.

"Sit up and drink this," he said in a voice that didn't encourage argument.

"I don't want to drink coffee." She pouted, moving restlessly on the bed. "Come on, McCabe, lie down and talk to me," she added with a coaxing, teasing smile.

"If I lie down with you, I won't talk." He caught her hand and jerked her up, leaning her against the pillows. He sat down beside her, grimacing with the movement, and handed her the coffee. "Drink it."

She moved it around in her hands, finding something oddly comforting in the hot ceramic in her hands. She lifted her eyes to McCabe's bare chest and felt herself going warm all over.

"I never liked Andy without a shirt," she said absently, sipping coffee while she stared. His chest rippled, as if he'd made an impatient movement. "You're..." She blinked, trying to find a word to describe it. "Sexy," she said triumphantly, lifting her eyes.

Whatever she expected to see in his face, it wasn't pain. But he was almost white with it, and the sight was more sobering than the coffee.

"Your leg," she said softly. "Oh, McCabe, your poor leg. And I didn't even think, and you were walking without your cane!"

"My leg is all right," he said coldly.

"Oh, sure it is, that's why you look so happy," she shot back. Her head felt dizzy. She set the coffee cup down gently on the bedside table. "Go back to bed, why don't you? I'm all right. I'm quite through throwing myself at you for tonight."

She said the words with bitter humor, suddenly realizing what the alcohol had done to her. And she'd taken off her blouse and her bra! She went a bright red and stiffened against the pillows.

"I certainly hope so," he said quietly. "I don't think I could take any more."

There was a curious silence around them, and it forced her eyes up to his. They were glittering under his thick lashes, and something about the stillness of his body, the expressionless mask of his face, frightened her.

Almost as if he couldn't help it, his hand went toward her gown where ten pearl buttons fastened it from collarbone to waist. He looked down at his own big callused hands and watched as his fingers unlooped the first, then the second, the third...

Wynn was too shocked to say anything. At first she even thought it might be a hallucination brought on by the alcohol. But when he peeled the gown away from her breasts and sat staring at them, she realized it was no dream.

Unconsciously her body lifted, an involuntary kind of pleading as the hunger in his darkening eyes touched it.

She looked down, too, shocked by what was happening. He didn't touch her. He didn't even try. But his eyes ate every creamy inch of her, right up to the hard, taut peaks that betrayed the longing she couldn't hide.

It was incredible, to lie here like this and let him see her as no other man ever had, and not to protest. Where was her mind?

His eyes wandered back up to hers and searched them. It was an exchange that left her trembling. She'd never seen a pair of eyes look like that, burn like that. She couldn't bear to hold his gaze but she couldn't look away. She felt as if she had a live wire in her hand and couldn't turn it loose. And her heart was throbbing, and she wanted him to touch her more than she wanted to take another breath.

His chest rose and fell heavily. She could see the pulse in his strong, tanned throat like a triphammer. It was a moment out of time when words would have been an intrusion.

Very gently he took her shoulders and drew her up against his broad bare chest, closing his arms around her very slowly, so that her taut breasts were cushioned in the thick hair over his warm muscles. She held her breath while it was happening, too shocked and awed to breathe. Her cheek slid softly against his as he drew her even closer until her bareness was warming his. His big arms enfolded her as if she were a breakable treasure, and there was the faintest tremor in them. His face moved down to her throat and his lips pressed against her neck through the curtain of her hair, and he didn't say a word. He just held her, rocking her slowly, sweetly, against the warmth of him, while around them the night blazed up like a bonfire.

She let out her breath unsteadily at his ear and her hands held his head against her shoulder. It was unreal. Perhaps it really was the liquor. But it was beautiful, all the same. So beautiful and tender.

A long moment later, he drew back and searched her eyes, his body easing away from hers. Their skin clung slightly because of the dampness of their bodies, and she realized when the cool air washed over her that the gown had slipped to her waist without her even knowing it. He looked down at the soft bareness of her body one last time before he helped her back into the gown and slowly, deftly rebuttoned it.

Her lips parted, but his fingers pressed over them, and he shook his head and smiled softly, tenderly. He drew her hands to his chest and moved them over the hard muscles with a lazy indulgence, watching the expressions that crossed her face. He moved one hand onto the hard male nipple and let her feel its rigidity, and then smiled when he saw the surprise in her eyes. He guided her fingers to the rippling muscles above his belt buckle, and upward through the wedge of thick hair. Her lips parted and he leaned forward and kissed them, letting his lips open as they touched, letting her feel the texture of them without any pressure at all.

She could hardly breathe for the maelstrom of sensation he was creating. She gasped and he drew back.

His nose nuzzled hers, his lips brushed softly over hers, biting at them until her mouth opened hotly and begged for his. He gave it to her completely, hungrily, the strength and weight of him crushing her down into the mattress so that she could feel her breasts flatten achingly under it. Her nails moved restlessly against his chest and he moaned sharply. She hesitated, liking that reaction, and she did it again, harder this time, dragging them down to his belt and back up again. He lifted himself up to let her hands have total access to his torso, and she stroked him hungrily, feeling the muscles tauten and ripple under her hands, feeling the husky sigh of his breath.

But all at once he sat up, holding her down with one big hand flat on her belly when she would have followed him.

"No," he said. It was the first time he'd spoken since it all began, and his voice was oddly thick.

She swallowed, her lips hungry for his, her body aching in ways it was just discovering it could.

He looked big and dangerous, he looked like...like a lover must, she thought, studying the set of his head, the ripple of muscle as he got his breath.

His fingers touched her cheek, the one Andy had slapped, and his eyes were frankly murderous. "I'll break his jaw for that," he said quietly.

"He was hurt," she whispered.

"Not as much as he's going to be," he said flatly. "Nobody touches you that way."

He sounded possessive and protective, and she didn't understand why.

"You've had a shock tonight," he said, watching her, "and too damned much liquor to know what you're doing. So I'm not going to take advantage of it. But if you ever take off your blouse in front of me again, you won't get away so easily. I could take you, despite this damned leg, and I could get hot enough not to mind the pain. Do you understand?"

She averted her eyes. "I'm sorry. It was the alcohol."

He turned her head back to his. "No, darling, it wasn't the alcohol, not while you were letting me undress you. Your eyes were blazing with it."

"So were yours," she shot back with angry pride.

He only smiled. "I don't doubt it. Just looking at you nearly drove me over the edge. That's never happened before."

"You weren't drunk," she stated.

He shook his head. "No, I wasn't." He brushed her face with his fingers, studying every inch of it. "Why did you think I was in pain?"

"Your face was white," she said. "And you looked...so agonized."

"Haven't you ever seen a man eaten up with desire before?" he asked matter-of-factly.

That hadn't occurred to her. She turned beet red and dropped her eyes to his chest. That was worse, because it brought back vivid memories of how it had felt to touch him there.

"No," she admitted after a minute.

"I feel like a man getting tangled in a net," he murmured, but when she looked up, he was only smiling.

"I don't want anything from you," she said shortly, remembering what he'd already said about ties.

"I want something from you, though," he said, letting his eyes wander down her body. "And if you pull that trick twice, I'll have it, too. All I have to do is touch you, and your body belongs to me."

"It does—" she began to deny it.

"And mine belongs to you," he added without a pause, catching her eyes. "You could see it tonight, couldn't you, the way I reacted when you touched me, here." He brushed his hands over his chest and his eyes darkened. "Did you feel what happened?"

She licked dry lips. "Yes," she said, remembering the tautening muscles, the sound that had been dragged out of him.

"I wanted you tonight, Wynn," he said. "I wanted you obsessively, and because of that I'm going to get on a plane tomorrow and fly up to New York for the weekend. I'm going to put some space between us until we cool off."

"I won't seduce you," she said bitterly.

"You could," he said, watching her. "Did you know that? You could seduce me just by walking into the room and touching me."

That shocked her, and he nodded when he saw the betraying wideness of her eyes.

"So, that being the case, I feel like a brief vacation." He got up and moved slowly away from the bed toward the door.

"McCabe, I'm sorry about what I told Andy," she said quietly. "And about...about what I did to you."

He turned, lifting an amused eyebrow. "Don't apologize for it. I can't think of a time in my life when I've been so aroused so fast, I'd almost forgotten that I was a man."

She swallowed hard, because it embarrassed her to have him admit such a thing. "I didn't mean to."

He stared across the room at her. "I've had any number of careless encounters over the years," he mused, studying her. "But I can't remember anything as erotic as what we just did together, do you know that?"

Her eyes widened, softened. "Me either," she admitted.

"Ah, but you're a virgin," he reminded her. "I'm not."

She hated the very thought of those other women, and it showed.

"Jealous?" he chided.

"Not me, mister," she assured him. "I wouldn't tie a single string to you."

"And that's a lie." He grinned. "You wanted me. I felt it."

Her chest rose and fell roughly. "Well, you weren't Mr. Cool yourself!"

"That's a fact." He let his eyes linger on her full breasts. "It drives me wild, thinking you've never been looked at or touched intimately before. I keep wondering how it would be with you, the first time." His eyes shot up to hold hers, and she felt her heart bursting in her chest at the intensity of his look. "In that bed you're lying in right now, Wynn," he said huskily. "Your body and mine with nothing between us, and the cool night air washing over us while we made love...."

"Go away!" she whispered.

"I am," he reminded her. "And now you know why."

He closed the door softly behind him, and

the next morning the local taxi service carried him off to the airport, leaving a subdued Wynn behind to spend the most miserable weekend of her life alone.

Chapter Seven

Andy didn't call. Not that Wynn expected him to. But it was the first weekend she'd spent totally alone since they'd gotten engaged.

Worst of all was that she missed McCabe. She always had, ever since he'd left Redvale all those years ago, even though she hadn't admitted it before. She'd missed him, worried about him, brooded over him so that she hardly realized how fast the years were passing. When he didn't come back, and she'd secretly hoped that he would, she had had to face the fact that she could be alone for the rest of her life mooning over a man who had never so much as kissed her.

But now he had. And the desperation that had sent her eagerly into Andy's arms when he'd first proposed was back full force.

She wandered around, lingering helplessly in the room where McCabe slept because it was the only place in the house that was full of him. Not that she was snooping—she wasn't that kind of person. She didn't open drawers or look through his few things. But her eyes wandered over the bed he slept in, and glared at the battered suitcase he'd left behind with its multicolor stickers from all the countries he'd visited. And every time she remembered how it had felt to hold him and be kissed by him, she wanted to wail. It was going to make it so much worse when he left. No matter what she did with her life from now on, it was going to be pure hell, because she'd have the memories to eat her alive. It was better, in one way, when she hadn't experienced McCabe physically.

He didn't come back until late Sunday

night. Wynn heard the sound of a car, the slam of a door, and went to open the front door.

McCabe walked in, muttering something, with his duffel bag over one broad shoulder while he leaned heavily on the cane. He looked worn and tired, as if he'd been carousing all weekend. Wynn immediately thought of other women and what McCabe had said about being capable with women if he got involved enough, and she wanted to slap him.

But letting him know that wouldn't do. She had to be cool, so she smiled politely and asked about his trip.

"The mark of utter insanity, if you want to know," he told her flatly. "I'd forgotten how damned big that Atlanta airport is. You walk miles between concourse and ticketing—a man with a fleet of golf carts could open a concession and make a fortune there!"

"I'll bet New York was worse," she murmured.

"I flew into La Guardia," he told her. "It's a crackerbox compared with Hartsfield International. It's smaller than JFK and easier to get around, but I still feel as if I've had part of my thigh sawed off.''

He sat down heavily in the chair, rubbing his leg, with his disheveled head leaning back. ''Wynn, could you make me a cup of coffee?'' he asked wearily. ''And do you have an aspirin in the house?''

''I'll get them right now,'' she said without an argument.

Minutes later, when the aspirin was working and he'd finished his second cup of coffee and was smoking a cigarette, he studied her closely. She was wearing shorts and a green tank top, and his eyes went appreciatively up and down her slender legs.

''Been out?'' he asked politely.

''Yes,'' she said, neglecting to mention just where she'd been.

He took a draw from the cigarette. ''Has Andy forgiven you and come home?''

''Nope.''

His thick, dark blond eyebrows rose. ''But you've been out?''

''To carry the garbage,'' she said.

"Oh."

Her eyes involuntarily clung to him while she sipped her coffee. He was such an enormous man, she couldn't imagine how he'd ever managed to dodge bullets. Even now, the knit shirt he was wearing was straining against the powerful muscles in his chest and arms, and her stubborn mind insisted on wandering back to the night she'd touched them. That had been a revelation, because she'd never realized what a pleasure it was to experience a man's muscles in that particular way.

"I did a lot of thinking while I was gone," he said quietly.

"About what?"

He laughed shortly. "You know perfectly well about what." He shifted, grimacing as he shifted his legs. "About reorganizing your life for you, making things difficult." He stared at the tip of his cigarette. "I came down here with noble motives, Wynn. But I lost sight of them somewhere along the way."

She glanced at him warily. "Does that mean you're going to stop interfering?"

"Oh, not at all, darling," he drawled, smiling at her confusion. "As a matter of fact, I've decided that I was right in the first place. You need Andy like a hole in the head. A man who'll knock a woman around is lower than a snake's belly."

She tended to agree with him; she'd never expected Andy to be that violent. But he hadn't done it without provocation. "It was my fault, you know," she said. "I provoked him by telling him I was sleeping with you."

"I can understand that," he said. "I'd have felt the same way if you'd told me he was your lover. But I wouldn't have hit you."

"No," she agreed. "Probably you would have kissed me, the way you did Friday night."

He searched her face quietly, and the room was suddenly alive with tension and remembered passion. "That backfired on me, didn't it?" he murmured. "I never meant to get so involved."

She felt herself go hot, because she'd been the same way, utterly out of her head.

He nodded. "Yes, it was the same for you, wasn't it? Two sane people who touch each other and go mad."

Her lips parted. "I...I have my own life here and I like it. I don't want to...complicate it."

"You don't want to sleep with me," he interpreted. "Why?"

Her eyes fell. "Because I couldn't survive it."

"At the moment, I'm doubtful if I could either," he said, touching his thigh with a harsh laugh. "But with the right encouragement..."

She blushed to her hairline and stood up. "I need to get some sleep. Mondays are rough, remember? I imagine you could use a little rest, too."

He got to his feet and stood in her way as she started past him. "I missed you," he said shortly. "I didn't like that—missing someone."

"Join the club," she said with a nervous laugh.

"Wynn, are you in love with Andy?" he asked quietly.

She drew in a steadying breath; he was much too close. "No," she admitted.

Relief washed away some of the lines from his face. "Afraid of me?" he asked, studying her eyes closely.

"Oh, you do terrify me, all right," she said facetiously, but it was the truth.

He sighed heavily. "Yes, I realize that. It isn't making things easier."

She went into her room and closed the door before she weakened and threw herself onto his big body and begged him to love her.

Monday was always frantic, the last full day to gather news and ads, since the press deadline was at noon on Tuesday. Wynn covered a visit from the lieutenant governor of the state, who was in Redvale to see firsthand the necessity for the mayor's proposed watersystem expansion. By the time she'd driven to the airport, followed him around with the camera and taken pictures and then got back to the office to write the story, the piece had already taken all morning. There had been other reporters covering the story as well, from neighboring towns, and she had had to wait her turn to get to the politician.

"I want this ready by the deadline too," McCabe said curtly, tossing a page of badly typed copy at her. "Rewrite it while you're at your desk."

She glanced at it and frowned. "This is a suicide," she told him. "Ed doesn't run suicides."

"Ed isn't here."

"McCabe, it's rough enough on the family—"

"It's news. Print it." And he got up and walked heavily out of the room, cane in hand.

She did the political story first and then fiddled and fumed around with the suicide story until she'd written it in such a manner that it didn't read like a suicide at all. She'd noticed that the sheriff's department was still investigating the facts surrounding the man's death, so she smugly stated that he had died of unknown causes.

McCabe, having taken the story over the phone, was, naturally enough, interested to read the final version. And when he did, he exploded.

"It wasn't of unknown causes, unless you call a bullet through the brain mysterious," he growled at her, slamming the copy down on her typewriter, his gray eyes blazing.

"This is a small town," she shot back, rising to battle. "You're only here to recuperate, but I live here twenty-four hours a day, and so do Ed and the rest of the staff. You may be a big-time journalist, and the manner of a man's death may not mean that much to you, but here it's a matter of honor. Did you even notice his last name?" she added, gesturing toward the copy. "I don't know him personally, but his family is one of the oldest and finest in the community. When we needed a city park, they donated land. When there was a charity drive, they gave hundreds of dollars. When the Burnes family was burned out, they gave them a home until they could find a new one. Those are special people, McCabe, and I can't see trading on their tragedy to fill a hole on your front page.'' She got up from the desk. ''If you want to run it, go ahead, but you rewrite it and please add your byline. And if you do run it you can have my resignation on the spot. I'd rather go hungry than be accused of promoting sensationalism.''

He was watching her with narrowed eyes. ''And this is exactly why I never wanted you connected with reporting,'' he said. ''You're too soft, Wynn. You care too much.''

''Isn't that better than being dead inside?'' she returned hotly. ''I try my best to be objective, McCabe, and I never take sides. But I can't see capitalizing on tragedy.''

''It's news, you little mule,'' he told her. ''News. That comes first in this business, not personal feelings and misgivings. We aren't here to censor it, we're here to present it to the public.''

''Ah, but there's another angle,'' she told him. ''Ed says there's a fine line between the public's right to know and the public's need to know. If it was a violent murder, I wouldn't argue, because knowing about it might protect someone from having it happen to them. But a man's suicide, done quietly, for deeply personal reasons...how do you fit that in with the public's need to know?"

He blinked. "It's news."

"Suppose it was your mother?"

He actually winced.

"You've been in international journalism too long," she said quietly. "You've forgotten how it is in small towns. I meant it. If you print this—" she picked up the story "—I'll go right out the door. And tomorrow's Tuesday."

He drew in a deep breath. "That's blackmail. And I oughtn't to let you get away with it." He lifted his chin arrogantly. "But if you feel that strongly about it, I'll back down this once." He emphasized the last two words. "In the meantime, you remember that I'm editing this paper, and I'll do it my way."

"Yes, McCabe," she said with a sweet, demure smile.

He caught her chin and planted a hard,

rough kiss on her startled mouth. Fortunately there was no one to see it, but Wynn blushed anyway.

"Not bad," he murmured with a faint smile. "But it's better when you open your mouth and kiss me back in that slow, hot way you did in your bedroom."

"McCabe!" she burst out, putting a hand over his mouth before anyone could hear him.

He kissed her palm and turned away. "All right, you're safe in here. Too many witnesses," he added from the doorway.

She sat down heavily and stared after him. Well, she'd expected him to get his own back. But she'd won. She threw the story into the trash can.

But if she'd expected that that was all the revenge McCabe meant to take, she was badly mistaken. Later that afternoon, there was a bank robbery. Wynn, sitting at her desk, heard it come over the police scanner and automatically opened the filing cabinet to pull out her camera and strobe light.

She was putting her pad and pen into her purse when McCabe walked in.

"Where are you off to?" he asked.

"There's a bank robbery in progress at Farmer's Bank," she burst out. "I'm on my way."

"Oh, no, you're not!" he growled, taking the camera away from her. "Sit down."

"McCabe!"

"Sit down, I said!" he barked harshly, forcing her down into the chair. "Bank robbers carry guns, you little fool!"

"McCabe, it's my job," she said. "It's what I do!"

"Not when I'm here, it isn't." He looked oddly pale. "You sit there and listen on the scanner. When the action's over, call the police and get the story. You can go down and get pix of them carrying him off to jail, if you like, when they make an arrest, and you can interview the bank staff and get pix of them. But you don't leave this office while it's going down, do you understand?"

"Ed would let me go!" she flashed.

"Ed couldn't stop you." His face was set into rigid lines, and for the first time since he'd been back, she saw the man underneath the careless, easygoing mask. She saw right through to the steel that had carried him through all the years in the front lines.

"Now, stay put," he said shortly. "Or would you like to spend a few weeks in the hospital with a bullet through you? Maybe I should have let you change this bandage after all," he added, his gray eyes flashing wildly. "Do you know how big a hole a pistol makes?"

"I...thought you were shot with a rifle," she faltered.

"I was shot at point-blank range with a pistol," he told her flatly. "And except for a friend in the junta who knocked the guard's arm and then helped me escape, it would have been through the head. I was being executed for trying to save those other journalists."

She burst into tears as the impact of what he'd confessed hit her. She sat there trembling all through her body and feeling as if a part of her was dying of terror.

"Now, you know," he said with a cold

smile. "So don't get adventurous, will you darling? Being shot is a sobering experience." And he turned and went back out, closing the office door behind him.

She hardly heard the scanner at all. She couldn't seem to stop crying. McCabe was being executed, executed, executed... If not for that soldier, he'd be dead now, and she'd never have held him, kissed him, touched him. It was a nightmare that she couldn't escape and she didn't know how she was going to stay sane if she kept thinking about it. Because she was in love with him. Horribly, hopelessly in love with him. And when he was healed, he was going to climb on a plane and fly straight back to that other world, that bloody world where his life was at risk every second. And she knew she'd never survive the fear again. It was one thing to worry about a man she'd hero-worshiped, quite another to worry about a man she loved, knowing there'd never be another man she'd want or need so much. He'd given her a glimpse of his own private hell just now, and she'd fallen in head-first.

Ten minutes later, Kelly burst into the room, all eyes. "I just heard about the robbery on my scanner," he said excitedly. "They've made an arrest. Can I go...would you mind? I'll get good pix, honest I will."

Wynn handed him the camera like a zombie. "Don't forget to roll the film after each shot," she said dully.

"Sure, I won't forget this time." He paused at the doorway. "You okay?"

She nodded. "Interview the bank people, too, Kelly."

"Will do! See you later."

And he was gone like a shot. She finally dragged herself back together and finished her stories. It was time to go home before McCabe came back into the room, and he studied her for a long time before he spoke.

"Let's go home," he said quietly.

She nodded, getting up from her desk and gathering her purse. She followed him out, calling good-bye to the others woodenly.

After a meal that neither of them seemed to enjoy, McCabe went off into the living room to watch the news and Wynn took a bath and finished a dress she'd been sewing for days. She called good night to McCabe without having spoken to him at all, and went to bed.

She went to sleep early, emotionally exhausted, and found herself sitting straight up in bed hours later as a wild, harsh cry woke her.

She blinked, listening in the darkness. The window was open, but when she looked at the moonlit night outside, she didn't see anything. The sound came again, louder. And she suddenly realized that it was coming from McCabe's room.

Wynn got out of bed in her thin blue cotton gown and didn't stop to grab a robe. She burst into McCabe's room without even knocking and found him thrashing like a madman on the crisp white sheets. The cover had long since been kicked away, and he was nude. But she was past embarrassment, pushed there by the horror in his voice.

"McCabe," she said, shaking him as she sat down beside him on the bed. "McCabe, wake up!"

It might not have been the thing to do when a person was having a nightmare, but she couldn't bear to hear the raw terror in his deep voice as he cried out.

She shook him again, harder, and he jerked upright, his eyes open wide, so that in the moonlight they looked pagan and fierce.

He caught his breath sharply and there was a strange glitter in his eyes, a moisture.

"Oh, God," he ground out, shaking. "God!"

He put his head in his hands and breathed roughly. "Oh, Wynn, someday I'm afraid I won't wake up in time..."

She put her arms around him and drew his shaggy head down on her shoulder. Her hands soothed him, stroking his head gently. "It's all right," she said softly. "You're safe. You're safe, McCabe."

His own arms went around her with a heavy sigh and he held her, shaking and damp with sweat, his heart thundering.

"Did I wake you?" he asked wearily. "I'm sorry. I don't often have nightmares like this, but I've been told I get pretty loud."

Told by whom? she wondered with a wild flare of jealousy. But this wasn't the time or place for that. He was in trouble and everything womanly in her reached out to help.

His hands bit into her back. "I shouldn't have told you what I did this afternoon, about how I got shot," he said unexpectedly. "I regretted it the minute the words were out, but I was so afraid that you'd get in the line of fire…"

She felt her breath catch. "You were afraid…for me?"

"No, for the bank robbers," he ground out angrily. His hands flattened on her back and seemed to savor the warmth of her body under the thin gown. "Of course, for you."

"I've done it before," she whispered.

"That's what frightened me so, thinking you had." His head nuzzled against her neck, her shoulder. His hands moved up and down lazily at her back, causing sensations that were faintly shocking.

"I can take care of myself—isn't that your favorite line?" she asked with a laugh.

"So I keep saying." He was still getting his breath back. "That was one hell of a nightmare."

Her hands soothed him. "McCabe, tell me about it."

"No." He held her tight for an instant before he let her go and slid back down onto the pillows with a hard sigh. "All that thrashing around knocked the bandage loose. Wynn, will you faint if I turn on the light?"

She felt a jolt go through her body, but she said weakly, "No."

He reached out, and light flooded the room. He propped himself against the headboard and grimaced as he looked down. "Damn."

She followed his gaze, almost losing her poise entirely as her eyes passed over his nudity with helpless wonder. He was...perfect.

But when she saw the wound, the extent of it, she lost her self-consciousness. "Oh, McCabe, no wonder it hurts so," she ground out, gritting her teeth at the discoloration and the marks where the stitches were.

"They told me it was going to be a while

before I'd feel like running races," he said.
"Now you know why. Can you rebandage it?
I'll even pull the sheet over my hips while
you're gone."

"Thanks a lot," she managed, getting to her
feet without glancing his way, her face so
bright it could have lit the way through a bliz-
zard.

When she came back, armed with antiseptic
and fresh bandages from the medicine cabinet,
he had the sheet over his narrow hips and was
watching her with eyes that were faintly
wicked.

"I wish I'd had a camera," he murmured,
watching her go to work efficiently and silently on the wound. "That was an enlight-
ening experience."

"I'm trying to think of it as a forced anat-
omy lesson," she muttered.

He only laughed, watching her deal with the
wound. She put on the fresh bandage and
taped it in place, trying not to enjoy the feel
of his hard-muscled thigh under her slender
fingers.

He was studying her, his eyes going to the bodice of the nightgown. It would be the same one he'd unbuttoned several nights back, she thought miserably.

"If Katy Maude could see this, she'd faint dead away," Wynn said unsteadily.

"You told Andy we were lovers," he reminded her. "And I told him the same thing."

Her eyes jerked up. "You did what?"

"I went to see him," he said with malicious pleasure.

"Oh, McCabe, you didn't hit him?"

He stared at her. "After what he did to you? My God, what kind of man would I be to let him get away with that? Of course I hit him!"

She felt as if the roof had fallen on her. "It didn't occur to you that he'll spread gossip all over town about us now?"

"It occurred to me."

"And it didn't bother you one bit, either, did it?" she grumbled. "You'll be off in a few weeks, and why should you care about my reputation?"

"I care a great deal about it," he said. "Too much."

"Well, don't lose sleep over it," she grumbled. "I'll survive."

She put aside the antiseptic and sat up straight. She didn't want to look concerned, but she couldn't help it. "Will you sleep now?"

"It's just a bad dream, honey," he said.

"Not if you keep having it." She folded her hands in her lap. "You asked me who I talked to about the job. Who do you talk to, Mc-Cabe?"

"I'm a man," he said.

"You're not invulnerable," she replied. "There's no shame in fear, is there? It's a human thing."

"I suppose that most people with a pistol against their temples would feel fear," he agreed. He settled himself more comfortably into the pillows. His fingers rubbed at his eyes for a minute, as if to clear them. "I've been in tough situations before, but I think that's the closest to death I've ever come. I dream about it all the time, except that when I dream, there's no friendly soldier there to save me."

She caught one of his big hands in hers and held it on the bed, savoring its callused warmth, its strength. "Tell me about it."

"Are you sure, Wynn? It's not a pretty story."

"I'm sure."

So he told her about where he'd been. About the fighting and the slaughter and the hopelessness of the people. About the children lying dead in the streets and the native journalists who were put to death if they dared to print anything unfavourable to the regime. About the danger foreign journalists placed themselves in when they went there, and the ones who'd been killed already. About the poor peasants murdered and left on the sides of the roads without even the dignity of burial. And then, slowly, reluctantly, about the death of his friends and how it had been when the soldiers took him out of the small, stifling rock building with the dirt floor, and one of their number had put a pistol to his head.

His hand tightened on hers. "You always think you're ready to die," he said. "Then it comes down to it, and all you can get in your mind is how many things you've left undone. You were one of my loose ends, Wynn. That's why I came back.''

"Loose ends?'' she murmured.

"I've played the heavy authority figure with you since your father died. By long distance, anyway. I wrote, and I talked to you on the phone and remembered to send cards on special occasions. But,'' he sighed, ''I never really thought about how alone you were, even with Katy Maude for company. I knew I had to come back, spend some time with you, really get to know you. Then when I spoke to Ed and heard you were about to marry Andy...I got on the first plane.''

"Why did it bother you?''

"I don't know,'' he said honestly. He looked up into her eyes and frowned. ''It shouldn't have. Andy wasn't any worse than any other man, on reflection. Until he slapped you,'' he added menacingly, and his eyes flashed. ''But I didn't like the thought of your being married. You're so young, Wynn.''

"I feel pretty ancient, if you want to know," she told him.

"Do you? I feel that way myself sometimes. Mostly when I'm with you," he added with a faint smile.

"I'm back in the nursery again, I gather," she said resignedly.

"Is that how I sounded?" His fingers curled into hers, nudging them apart sensuously to lock between them. "I'm all too aware that you're a woman, Wynn." He looked up into her eyes. "And you're very much aware of the effect you have on me, aren't you?"

"Yes," she admitted, avoiding his eyes.

"If you were a few years older and more sophisticated, I'd take you to bed, and get you out of my system," he said flatly. 'But that isn't possible. So I think it might be a wise idea if you got out of my room, darling, before I throw off this sheet and drag you in here with me."

She stood up, disengaging her hand. "I appreciate your efforts on my behalf," she murmured.

"What do you want me to do, Wynn, marry you?" he burst out furiously. He sat straight up, and his eyes glittered. "Wouldn't that be a colossal mistake, with you in one country and me in another? Because I won't give it up. It's my life."

"I know that," she agreed. "Where would you get the raw material for those sleazy books you write without it?" she added sarcastically.

"They aren't sleazy," he said coolly. "They're adventure novels. And I don't need to poke my nose into military coups to write them."

"Then why do it at all?" she demanded.

"Because someone has to! Someone has to get the word out, so that truth and freedom aren't totally suppressed!" he shot at her.

"And you're the only reporter who can do that, of course," she said calmly.

"I love my work, Wynn. I always have. And I told you, I don't need ties."

"So you did. But I do. And since I'm not likely to find anybody I like better than

Andy," she said defiantly, lying through her teeth, "I'm going to make it up with him. You just go back to your jungles and get yourself killed. I'll marry Andy and sleep with him and have his babies."

"I'll kill him first!" he said passionately.

She jumped at the soft violence in his voice, at the fervor, and stood with her back to the door gaping at him.

He threw off the sheet and got to his feet, devastatingly male, without a stitch of clothing on his big body. Mindless of her embarrassed shock, he walked toward her, pausing when he was close enough to back her up against the door.

"I'm too old," he began hotly, "to be remodeled or renovated. I am not changing professions and I am not marrying you."

"I haven't asked you to," she said reasonably. "Will you please put on your pants?"

"No, you can get used to seeing me naked. "Think of it as sex education. Now, listen to me, Wynn," he said hotly. "There's no reason for you to jump into marriage with a man who's physically violent."

"That's exactly right," she agreed. "That's why I wouldn't marry you on a bet."

He drew in an angry breath. "Not me, Andy!"

"Andy was only violent because I told him you were a wonderful lover," she explained.

He stopped ranting and stared down at her. His chin lifted slightly and he frowned. "Did you?"

She nodded. "Umhmmm." Her eyes searched his. "What kind of lover are you, McCabe?" she asked in a husky, strange voice as his nearness and disreputable appearance began to work on her bloodstream.

His nostrils flared. "Want me to show you, Wynn?"

Her eyes dropped to his broad chest and she wanted to say yes with all her heart. But thinking about the consequences was enough to make her shake her head. She couldn't risk it. Losing him was going to be traumatic enough without the complication of intimacy.

"No," she said on a weary breath. "No, it's better if I never know. Good night, McCabe."

"Wynn?"

His voice sounded odd, but she refused to meet his eyes. "Yes?"

"You'll find someone...a man who'll be able to give you what you want."

Did he know, she thought with terror, did he realize that she loved him? She finally met his gaze, uncertainty and apprehension in her eyes, and he searched them slowly.

"I'm not domesticated," he said in a husky voice.

"I haven't said a word," she reminded him. "You do what you like, McCabe. If you want to get killed, go ahead."

"The way I die is up to God," he reminded her hotly. "It could happen here just as easily as it could happen overseas, and you know it!"

That was true, but knowing it didn't help. "Yes, that's probably true. And now that you mention it," she added, wanting to goad him, "I've always wondered what it would be like to work for the wire services."

His face actually paled. "Oh, no, you don't," he began.

"I'm over twenty-one," she reminded him, though she had no real intention of making good on her threat. "I can do what I like. Yes, I think I might like being a foreign correspondent. But the Middle East would be more interesting to me. I could see the pyramids. What a wonderful idea!"

He exploded at the smile on her face, the perverse light in her eyes. "No way, Wynn. I'll stop you!"

"How?" she asked calmly.

He blinked, as if the question caught him off guard, and just stared at her.

"You'd better get some rest, and so had I," she told him. "Tomorrow is press day. Good night, McCabe, sleep well."

And she turned, careful not to look down, and shut the door behind her. She could hear him cursing roundly as she started down the hall to her own room, and she smiled. Let him chew on that possibility for a while and see how he liked it!

Chapter Eight

The next morning McCabe looked like a volcano about to erupt. Under the close-fitting tan slacks and beige patterned shirt he was wearing, hard muscles rippled as he moved around the kitchen. Wynn watched him helplessly, remembering the one quick glimpse she'd had of him last night, all man, all muscle and grace.

"You are not going to join the wire-service staff," he told her without any attempt at civility, glaring at her across the table while she nibbled toast and sipped coffee.

Her eyebrows rose. "I'm not?"

"Don't give me that big dumb look of yours," he said curtly. "It won't work." He checked his watch. "We don't have time to sort things out today, but tomorrow, lady, you and I are going to have a talk."

She finished her toast. "No, we're not. You have a planning-commission meeting tomorrow morning and an industrial-authority meeting tomorrow afternoon," she said sweetly. "You promised Ed."

Irritation claimed every line of his face. "Just what I need," he muttered. "Small-town progress."

Her green eyes glittered at him. "You used to be part of this town," she reminded him. "And the way we're beginning to grow is no joke to those of us who love our community. We were on the way to extinction before our city fathers decided to band together and go out after industry. This town matters to me, McCabe. My children are going to grow up here."

He lifted his head and stared at her for a long moment, and an odd expression touched his gray eyes as they wandered over her face.

She pushed her chair away from the table. "But, as you say, there's no time for discussion. It's press day." She groaned. "Maybe I'll just quit right now and save myself the bother of doing it around two o'clock like I usually do."

"It's interesting, making up a paper again," he said, rising. "It's been a long time."

"'Interesting' is not the best word for it," she told him.

And by two o'clock he was agreeing with her, as he helped answer phones between efforts to cut and paste copy onto the front page. He was trying to write headlines at the same time, and write out correction lines for Judy to set at the typesetting computer, and make up last-minute ads. And his leg was giving him trouble; Wynn could see it in the drawn lines of his face. Everybody stood to make up the paper; it was almost impossible to do it sitting down, even in the high chairs that were used at the light table to make up printing jobs and mask negatives.

She got one of those chairs and eased it in

front of the makeup board where the front page was lying. He glowered at her as he turned from the waxer with another strip of copy in his hand.

"It will be easier," she said quietly. "And if you'll dictate the headlines to me and tell me what point type you want them in, I'll do them on the headline machine while Judy sets correction lines."

He sighed wearily. "All right, you win."

She picked up a scratch pad and a pen. "Okay. Shoot."

Time sped by, and there wasn't enough of it. There never was. But somehow they finished up and put the pages into the flat box, and Kelly rushed out the door with them on his way to the printer.

"I quit!" McCabe said shortly, rubbing his thigh with a big weary hand while Judy and Jess went through the jobwork to see what was pressing.

"Too late," Wynn told him. "You have to quit by two, or nobody listens to you."

He looked down at her, his eyes warm and

quiet and searching. "You're pretty," he said all of a sudden, studying her disheveled black hair, flashing emerald eyes and flushed complexion.

She caught her breath, because the compliment sounded genuine. "Am I?"

He nodded. One big hand moved to brush the hair away from her mouth, and he stared at it pointedly. "If you'll close the door," he whispered, "I'll make love to you."

She blushed and felt her cheeks go hot. "Oh, hush," she said sharply.

He smiled, the action making him seem younger. "Don't you want to be kissed, Wynn?" he asked, bending. "We do it so well together."

That was true, but he made her much too vulnerable to risk interludes like this.

"We'd better get home," she said. "I have to cover a city-council meeting tonight."

"Tonight?" he burst out.

"The city council meets the first Tuesday of every month. This is the first Tuesday."

He glared at her. "I was looking forward to

spending some time with you. When do you get home?"

"They're going to discuss the water system tonight. Probably I'll be lucky if they break up by midnight."

He looked furious, and she thought that it was probably a good thing the meeting would occupy her. He was too devastating at close range, and she was too vulnerable to him.

Her eyes went over his hard face. "Mc-Cabe, would you like to come with me?" she asked suddenly.

He almost laughed. "Do you think I'd find it entertaining?"

She turned away. "No, actually I thought you might find it interesting that we're achieving what was considered an impossible goal only a few months ago."

"Sorry," he said. "I deserved that. Yes, Wynn, I think I'd like to come with you."

Surprised and pleased, she walked out the door without letting him see her face.

They had a quick supper and went straight to city hall, and Wynn was frankly amused at the stares they got. Everyone knew McCabe was her house guest, but most of the people she dealt with hadn't seen him in years. The impact he had on the townspeople was fascinating.

Harry Lawson shook hands with him before the meeting was called to order.

"I hope you gave me front page on my water-system-expansion project," he told McCabe without preamble.

"As a matter of fact," McCabe told him, "I gave you a banner headline."

Harry grinned. "If you've already put the paper to bed, you may have to tear up your front page after this meeting," he confided. "I got a terrific piece of news late this afternoon. Tell you about it later."

Wynn's eyes widened. "He got the money he was counting on from the governor," she said with insight. "I'd bet half a week's pay."

McCabe glanced down at her as they eased into chairs near the front of the crowded room.

"You really are interested in this expansion, aren't you?"

"Yes, I am. Water is a serious issue these days, whether you've been in this country long enough to realize it or not." She looked up. "Everybody thinks we can't ever run out of it. But we can, McCabe. The water table is already dropping in many areas of the country, and the increased demand from municipalities and industry and agriculture is beginning to catch up with supply. What's going to happen when it exceeds it?"

He stared at her. "It can't happen here," he said hesitantly. "We've got two major rivers feeding our water supply."

"I think you ought to read that water study in my files," she told him. "It might surprise you to know that every drop of water in them both will have been allocated within ten years."

"My God!"

"You see the implications already, don't you?" she asked. "Towns will stop growing because industry needs water to operate. Subdivisions and housing complexes and apartment buildings will be curtailed for the same reason. Agriculture will be in trouble in times of drought.''

McCabe turned back toward the podium, where the mayor was calling the meeting to order. His eyes were interested for the first time, and he took in every word that was spoken, from the mayor's explanation to questions by the city council and visitors.

Wynn noticed that McCabe began taking notes, and he asked questions, too. She felt such a surge of pride in him that she could hardly contain it. He looked and sounded what he was—a formidable journalist with years of experience behind him.

The mayor's news was that the governor had allowed Redvale not the five thousand dollars it had asked for, but ten thousand. The governor had taken into consideration the town's desperate plight the year before, when drought had forced it to restrict water usage and ban watering gardens and washing cars and filling pools for the duration.

There was some serious debate and a few objections from taxpayers who didn't want to see the town go so far in debt for the expansion. Harry handled them well, though, and when the time came for a vote, the city council went unanimously for the project. It was on the way.

"What were you talking to Harry about after the meeting?" Wynn asked him as she headed the car toward home.

"Water," he confessed with a sideways grin. "I told him I'd be glad to do some public-relations work for him gratis if he needed it. It might make a good feature story for one of the national magazines," he added. "I'm going to check that out."

"You're super," she said quietly.

"I'm glad you think so. No, don't go home. Let's go get the front page and the editorial page back. I'll have to tear it up to make room for this story."

"I'd thought about asking you to hold the front page, but I wasn't sure the vote would go through," she said. "Ed doesn't like to hold it back, anyway."

"We'll make an exception this time. Wynn,

thanks for asking me to come with you," he said quietly. "I enjoyed it. Really...enjoyed it. I'm beginning to see that there are quite a few big challenges even in small towns."

She smiled to herself. She'd hoped that he would. McCabe loved a fight. And there were plenty of battles to wage right here.

It was midnight when they got back, having left the pages at the office to finish first thing in the morning and take back to the printer. It was a good thing the printer was an accommodating gentleman, Wynn thought with a smile, since they'd had to get him back to the office in the middle of the night to let them have those pages. But then, he was an old newspaperman himself, and understood.

Wynn had already started into her room when McCabe called her name softly in the dimly lit hall.

She turned and he hobbled up to her. "If you won't sleep with me, at least kiss me good night," he said deeply.

Her eyes searched his for a long time. "I was very proud of you tonight," she said, without meaning to.

He actually flushed. "I'm always proud of you," he replied. He rested the cane against the wall and drew her against him, spacing his legs so that she was drawn between them.

"McCabe!" she said nervously.

"I can't hold you against my legs," he said, his eyes searching hers. "I'm not trying to shock you."

"That would be something new," she murmured. The feel of his body was weakening her. She let her palms rest flat against his chest and her heart ran wild.

His hands linked behind her back at her waist and he lowered his forehead to rest against her own. "Wynn, you didn't really mean what you said about going back to Andy, did you?" he asked, as if it really mattered.

Her eyes closed. She could feel him, smell him. He was drowning her in scent and sensation and she rocked slowly against him.

"No," she whispered shakily, wanting nothing more than to lie in his arms and do all the things she'd dreamed of doing with him.

His lips parted and his breath came roughly. "I want to lie with you," he breathed against her mouth. "I want to lie with you and on you and under you, Wynn." His big hands slid up and down her back over the thin pink blouse she was wearing with her beige slacks. "Let me show you what you do to me." And he moved his hands down to the base of her spine and pushed her hips suddenly, shockingly against his.

She gasped, flushing wildly.

"I'm a man," he said unsteadily, watching her. "And I want you. I can't help it."

"I know that." He had sounded almost apologetic. And she felt a sense of guilt for causing him discomfort, even though there was no helping it.

"I can't have you permanently," he bit off. "But we could sleep together."

She shook her head, leaning it heavily against his shoulder as the feel of his hungry body made her stagger. "I couldn't bear it," she whispered. "You're already hurting, aren't you, McCabe?"

"My leg isn't," he murmured.

"That isn't what I meant, either," she murmured. "I may be innocent, but I'm not stupid. I know what happens to men when they… when they get like this."

His hands moved back up to her waist, relaxing their intimate hold on her, and he shuddered softly. "It's just an ache," he whispered. "The sweetest ache in the world, and I don't mind it. Not with you."

She drew back to look up at him, surprising a look on his face that she'd never seen, couldn't understand. "Is your leg bad?" she asked suddenly. "You've been on it most of the day."

"It's not so bad," he said. "But it's going to feel good to get off it," he confessed with a dry smile.

Her eyes searched his. "Will you be all right?"

He shook his head very slowly. "Not until I get you in my bed," he said bluntly.

She lowered her eyes to his chest. "I can't."

"Yes, you can!" he burst out, glaring at her. His hands caught the back of her head and held it while his mouth lowered onto hers with a crushing, demanding pressure. His lips forced hers open to meet the wild, sweet ardor of his mouth, and he kissed her until she moaned and clung.

"Wynn," he whispered, anguished, as his hands moved to her breasts and cupped them softly, warmly. "Oh, Wynn, Wynn, I've never wanted anyone so much!"

Her fingers brushed up and down over his shirt and moved to the buttons and trembled at the top one, toying with it while she struggled to get her breath.

"I want you, too," she managed. "But..."

"But, nothing," he said, sounding half-strangled.

"How would you manage it," she asked, feeling needed and wanted, "when you can't even bear to have your leg touched?"

"There are ways, and ways," he muttered. His eyes were charcoal dark and glittering with passion. "Take your clothes off, Wynn, and let me show you."

"You lecherous old thing," she retorted, drawing back. "I will not!"

"I'll bet you're beautiful," he said slowly, letting his eyes run up and down her body until it began to tingle from the scrutiny.

She caught her breath. "Hush," she said shortly. "You mustn't talk to me that way."

"It's all I can do, at the moment," he sighed bitterly. His eyes held hers and his lips parted under a rush of breath. His face was rigid. He looked big and blond and frankly dangerous. "We could undress each other," he said quietly. "And lie together, in my bed, in the light. We could make love in every sense except the ultimate one."

She swallowed. "And what would happen then?"

"We'd go to sleep, of course," he murmured, smiling.

"No, I meant what would happen then?" she said, staring up at him. "Do you really think that I could take that kind of intimacy with you in my stride, and pass it off as a pleasant interlude?"

He frowned slightly. "It's done all the time, Wynn."

"In your world, perhaps," she agreed. "Not in mine. You've been away a long time, you've grown away from the basics. But I haven't. In my world, intimacy is between man and wife, and it means something."

His eyes darkened as he studied her, unblinking. "And I was muttering about Andy's hang-ups," he said.

"Sorry to disappoint you, darling," she said sarcastically, "but I don't play that kind of bedroom game. And before you make some cutting remark, no, I don't expect you to offer me marriage for a few hours of fooling around."

He looked as if she'd hit him. His face colored slightly, and there was anger in his eyes, in the fingers that bit into her waist.

"You're making it sound like something cheap," he said flatly.

"Because that's what it is, McCabe," she replied quietly. "I don't think of sex as a pastime. Apparently you do."

"I've had to," he said surprisingly. "I haven't had the inclination or the opportunity to form any kind of lasting relationships with women."

"Yes, I can understand that."

His eyes searched hers. "I want to lie down with you and love you," he said softly. "Is that such a shameful thing?"

Her eyes closed and tears stung them. "No," she whispered. "But I couldn't bear having nothing but the memory of it, after you leave."

His hands stilled on her waist and she heard his breath go ragged. "What are you telling me?"

"That I'd rather not know how it feels to make love with you," she said tightly, "even in an incomplete way."

"Why?"

Her lips parted and she leaned against his broad chest, letting her forehead nuzzle him lovingly. "Because it would make it worse," she ground out, tired of subterfuge and games and lies. "I want you, all of you, with all my heart. But I can't live on bits and pieces of you, I'm too greedy. I can't be intimate with you and then watch you walk out of my life. It would tear me apart. It's bad enough already!''

His hands moved hesitantly to the back of her head and smoothed her hair gently. There was a fine tremor in those hard fingers that she didn't understand.

His head bent and she heard his soft, ragged breathing at her ear as his hands contracted and forced her cheek close against his broad, warm chest.

"What are you saying?" he whispered roughly.

She slumped, letting all the tension out in one unsteady breath as her eyes closed.

"I love you," she whispered.

Chapter Nine

He didn't speak. He seemed to stop breathing. The hands on the nape of her neck stilled and she felt his body tauten where it touched hers.

She hadn't realized how she'd been hoping that he'd be happy about her confession, that he'd tell her he felt the same and ask her to marry him and the future would be rosy and bright. But he didn't speak. And she felt rejection more sharply than any she'd felt in her life.

She drew away from him without actually looking at him, and laughed softly, nervously.

"Are you shocked, McCabe?" she chided. "Surely it must happen to you all the time. Women read those books you write. I'm sure this isn't the first time one of them threw herself at your feet."

He was watching her. Just watching her. And she was afraid to look up and see what might be in his eyes, because she couldn't bear pity.

"You needn't worry, I'm not going to threaten to throw myself under a train or anything," she said, moving to open her bedroom door. "I just thought it might make things easier if you understood the situation. I'm...very vulnerable with you. If you pushed the issue, I'd sleep with you. But I'd hate you, and myself, and I'd never get over it. So stop making passes, will you?" she added on an unsteady laugh. "Because it's all a game to you. But it isn't to me."

She turned away, but his hand caught her arm and gently turned her back.

"Wynn," he said softly, "it's no game."

And before she could protest, he lifted her

face to his and kissed her. It was like nothing she'd ever experienced in her life, not even with McCabe. She felt his mouth brush hers, part her lips, probe in a silence that was poignant with emotion. His hands brought her against his big body, his breath sighed out at her cheek, while he built the kiss into something that was worlds away from a touching of mouths. It was slow and fierce, but achingly tender, and she tasted him as she'd never dared.

"Does this feel like fun and games?" he whispered over her lips. "Do I feel like a man who's playing?"

Before she could get out an answer to the gruff question, he was kissing her again. She reached up, going on tiptoe to prolong the sweetness of the contact, feeling his body so rigid in unmistakable desire.

His teeth nipped her mouth and he grew rougher as the desire worked on him. His arms contracted, bruising her as he dragged her against him, letting her feel the full strength of the powerful muscles of his chest, his arms.

His tongue probed slowly, rhythmically into her mouth, and a harsh groan burst out of his throat.

He lifted his head, and she could see the turmoil in his face that she'd already felt in the tremor of his body.

"We'll get married," he said in a voice she hardly recognized. "Just as soon as I can get a license."

Her lips parted. "No."

"Yes." He bent and kissed her again, slowly, lazily, smiling when he felt her body lift to meet his.

"You...you'll just hate yourself," she whispered, "when the newness wears off, when you've had me." Her eyes were tortured. "I'd rather we just slept together...."

He shook his head. "Not yet."

"Your leg," she murmured, lowering her eyes. "I forgot."

'No, not my leg. My conscience." He lifted her chin. "I can't take you in my stride, either, Wynn. So we'll get married, and we'll see how it goes."

"And you'll rush right back off to Central America at the first opportunity," she said.

"I've already told you that I don't intend giving it up," he said curtly. "It's my life."

"Yes, I can see that," she said, her voice sad and bitter. "I won't marry you, McCabe. I won't stay here and try to work, worrying about whether or not you're going to die in some jungle covering a volleyball conflict."

"You want it all your own way, I suppose," he replied, his eyes glittering and blatantly unloverlike. He moved away from her to light a cigarette. "You want me to stay in Redvale and write books and forget all about it, is that how the song goes?"

"Chorus and verse," she returned. "I am not having babies alone."

"There *is* a hospital," he burst out.

"Big deal, and how about a husband to help me through it?" she asked him. "How about holidays and birthdays and anniversaries that I'll spend alone? How about weeks without letters or phone calls when you're incommunicado, and what will I tell the children? Yes, you have a daddy, here's his picture, and you'll actually get to see him between wars!''

He was looking more thunderous by the second. "Take me as I am, or leave me alone! I've told you once, I'm not changing. You're being unreasonable, Wynn, and you know it."

"I'm being unreasonable." She nodded, her green eyes blazing. "So what are you offering me, McCabe? A few nights rolling around in bed with you once or twice a year? Because that's all I'll get."

He made an angry gesture. "You're exaggerating it. You said you loved me! What kind of love is this?"

"The only kind I want," she said, calming. She studied his tanned face under its disheveled blond hair, and loved him until it hurt. "No deal, McCabe, I won't marry you, and I won't sleep with you. Andy may not be for me, but eventually I'll find someone else I can love enough to marry. A man who's willing to give as much as he takes."

He looked dangerous for an instant, his eyes charcoal gray and savage. "What are you giving?'' he taunted. ''Just your body and a profession of love?''

''The body is standard issue,'' she said. ''If you just want one for a night or two, may I suggest that you drive up to the city with a few fifty-dollar bills and stand on a street corner downtown?'' She moved into her room. ''On the other hand, my profession of love was a nasty mistake. You can forget I ever said it. As cheaply as you're treating it, it must not be worth much after all.'' And she closed the door on his shocked face and locked it.

She undressed and went to bed, ignoring the one sharp rap on the door and a puzzled deep voice calling her name softly. And surprisingly, she slept, too. She felt too numb to worry about the problem. It would hurt enough later.

McCabe was sipping coffee at the breakfast table when she went in. ''I poured you a cup when I heard you stirring,'' he said coolly. ''It should still be hot.''

He pushed it toward her as she sat down, and she noticed that he'd already added cream and sugar. She couldn't meet his eyes; she still felt the sting of embarrassment about her heartfelt outpouring of the night before.

"Do you want anything to eat?" she asked curtly.

"I'd choke to death trying," he said with equal bluntness. He sipped his coffee and put the cup down. "I'm going to finish out this week and go back to work."

She was expecting it, but it hurt just the same. Why did her eyes have to fill up with tears now?

"Did you hear me?" he ground out.

She took a slow breath and lifted her coffee to her mouth. She tried to speak, but couldn't, so she nodded.

"No argument?" He laughed sarcastically, his eyes narrow and glittering.

Her tongue came out to brush at a drop of coffee that had missed her mouth, and she shook her head jerkily.

She took another sip, but her hand was trembling so that she had to put the cup down again.

"Wynn, don't do this to me!" he said in a voice that was blatantly and involuntarily anguished. He got up from his chair and reached for her suddenly, dragging her up into his arms and holding her close enough to bruise her. He lifted her clear of the ground, mindless of the pain in his leg, trembling with violent emotion. His cheek scraped her skin, his mouth searching blindly for hers. He found it with a muffled groan and he kissed her and kissed her, tasting tears and feeling uncertain about where they came from.

"McCabe," she sobbed against his warm mouth. Her arms tightened around his neck as she kissed him back. "Your leg...!"

"Damn my leg," he breathed roughly. He bit at her mouth, teased it, forced it into a maelstrom of sensuality that had them both trembling with need.

She clung, loving him, showing him in all the ways she could. When he finally stopped and let her slide back down so that she could stand, he had to support her because she was too shaken to stand alone.

"I don't care if you leave," she whispered, her green eyes swimming in tears. "I don't care!"

"Yes, I can see that," he said unsteadily. He held her face in his big warm hands and kissed away every salty tear.

"It's not my fault," she ground out. "You didn't have to come back, you didn't have to ruin my life!"

"Yes, I did. Have to come back. The thought of you with Andy was killing me."

That was faintly shocking. She looked up and caught an expression in his eyes that knocked the question she meant to ask right out of her mind.

"And when I saw you again," he continued quietly, "I knew I'd never be the same. Wynn, I want to be free. But as long as you're alive, I'll never be free again."

The tears were back. He wasn't saying the words, but he was feeling them, and she could see them, actually see them, in his tormented face.

"Don't cry," he said softly. "You don't know how it hurts me to watch you."

She dabbed at her eyes with the backs of her hands. "I'm sorry I've made things hard for you," she said softly. "I won't interfere in your life anymore. I'll take what you can give and I won't ask for the moon. Okay?" She looked up at him with such love and trust in her green eyes that he groaned and bent to kiss her wildly.

"You made me feel like the worst heel God ever made," he ground out. "But I can't quit, Wynn, not...just yet. In a few years, maybe I can settle for small-town politics and writing books. But...not yet. I wish I could. I wish I could give you everything you want, the moon, the stars...a roomful of roses."

"All right," she said, capitulating totally.

"No argument?" he asked suspiciously.

She shook her head with a quiet, sad smile. "I love you," she said simply. Then her lower lip trembled and spoiled the whole effect.

His teeth ground together and he sighed. "Yes, I can see that," he said wearily, drawing her close. He rested his forehead against hers. "Wynn, marry me and we'll work out the details later. I can't live without you now. I've faced that squarely.''

She felt the same way, but he already knew that. She sighed and moved closer.

His lips moved from her forehead down to her mouth, and his hands moved from her waist up to her rib cage and he kissed her warmly, slowing, rocking her softly against him from side to side in a wildly erotic rhythm.

"McCabe?" she whispered, trembling.

"Shh," he whispered back. His hands moved down to her upper thighs, pressing them gently to his, even though the movement made him flinch a little. "Now lift up a little," he whispered, and caught his breath when she did.

She moaned sharply, her hands clutching at his shoulders as a sensation like nothing she'd experienced in her life made her shudder all over.

"Wynn!" he ground out, kissing her hotly, his mouth open, his tongue urgent.

She gave him back the kiss, feeling bound

to him by live electricity, crying out helplessly as she burned with frustrated longing.

His hands were under the knitted blouse she was wearing, moving on her bare back to unfasten her frilly little bra. They moved around her, lifting softly, cupping, teasing, until she thought she'd never breathe normally again.

"Lie down with me on the couch," he said unsteadily, moving her toward it with a hard hand on her arm.

She didn't say a word, or protest. She eased down into the soft cushions and watched him strip off his shirt before he stretched out beside her.

Her green eyes widened at the expression on his face as he arched over her, and her fingers trembled as she lifted them to smooth over his broad, warm chest. He was perspiring just a little, and the curling hair that covered the powerful muscles was faintly damp under her caressing hands.

He trembled as she touched him, lifting himself up to give her hands enough space, watching her, letting her see how it affected him.

"I love to touch you," she whispered achingly.

"I love to touch you, too," he returned, his voice deep and gentle. He eased down on his elbow and tugged at her blouse. "Take it off, Wynn."

She hesitated for an instant, and he tugged at it again, smiling.

"I've seen you before," he reminded her. "And you've seen me—all of me. We're going to be married. So doesn't that give us a few privileges?"

They were and it did. So she sat up and let him help ease the blouse and bra away and then she stretched back out and let him look.

His fingers traced the silken skin around her full breasts lightly, appreciatively, while his eyes got drunk on the sight of her.

"Have you ever thought about what it would feel like if I kissed you here?" he asked, touching the soft swell lightly.

Her eyes widened and she breathed unsteadily. "Oh, yes, I've thought about it," she confessed.

He bent his head with a faint smile and brushed his open mouth across her creamy skin, dragging it sensuously back and forth until she arched up toward him with a sharp cry.

"I like that," he murmured. His hands slid under her shoulders to hold her where he wanted her, while his mouth took absolute possession of every taut line and curve of her.

She shuddered helplessly. It was the most incredible kind of pleasure, and she clung to him, holding his head, his mouth, against her.

"I said the first time I kissed you that you were passionate," he murmured, lifting his head at last to look into her shocked eyes. "But I didn't know the half of it, did I, darling? Sweet and wild in my arms, as abandoned a lover as any man could want."

"We...aren't lovers," she whispered.

"Not yet," he murmured, bending to kiss her tenderly. "Soon. Very soon, we will be. And I'll show you all the slow, intimate ways a man and woman talk to each other with their bodies."

Her eyes searched his. "You're very good

to look at, without your clothes," she said hesitantly.

He smiled delightedly at the shy little observation. "I imagine you look very good without your own, from what you've let me see." His hand smoothed down over the skirt she was wearing and the smile faded. "Wynn, will you let me undress you?"

She could hardly get her breath at all. She went wild, thinking how it would be to let him smooth away the skirt and her hose and her brief little lacy underthings, and really see her, all of her, with those dark, patient eyes. Her lips parted at the sensations that wound up in her and exploded.

She reached up and touched his chest, letting her hands find their way down to his hard waist and the muscular stomach at his belt buckle. He stiffened at her touch and silently took her hands and urged them under the belt, under the fabric, to the flat, muscular plane of his stomach.

She felt him shudder and her eyes widened. "Oh, McCabe," she whispered, awed.

The innocent movement of her fingers seemed to trigger something violent in him.

His body crushed down over hers deliberately and he held her eyes while his lips settled exactly over hers and his long, powerful legs insinuated themselves intimately between her own.

His forearms caught most of his weight, but he was still heavy enough to crush her down into the cushions. She looked straight into his eyes and gasped helplessly at the fiery arousal he was letting her feel.

"When we get married, Miss Ascot," he said roughly, "this is how we're going to lie in my bed. But there won't be acres of fabric between us, and you'll be able to feel every inch of me burning down into your body."

Her lips opened as she stared at him, drowning in the feel and smell and heat of him. "Isn't this hurting your leg?" she whispered in a stranger's voice.

"Unbearably, darling," he confessed, but there was something hot and wild blazing in his eyes. "And I don't even feel it. All I feel is you. You, Wynn, like silk and flame, and I want you until I could strip naked and run into a forest fire without feeling the heat.''

Her fingers touched his face, tenderly for all the fierce emotion she felt. ''Then, take me, if you need to,'' she whispered. ''I'll let you.''

He swallowed, and his eyes dropped to her lips. ''I want to,'' he said. ''But I don't think I can.''

Her eyes mirrored her amusement about that, and he managed a smile, too.

''That's not what I meant, Wynn,'' he murmured deeply. ''As you can feel, I'm perfectly capable right now. What I meant is, I don't think I want to spoil things.''

Her misty eyes questioned him and he laughed self-consciously and brushed the disheveled dark hair away from her face.

''It's different, somehow,'' he said slowly. ''I never used to mind taking women to bed, but it's special now. I want you in white satin walking down the aisle. I want the whole world to know that you didn't toss your principles down the drain and go promiscuous even when the rest of the world did.'' He frowned slightly, watching her. ''And I want it in a church, even if we just have a small ceremony. I want everything proper and aboveboard. And that doesn't include anticipating it on this sofa,'' he added on a sigh, rolling away from her to lie heavily on his back.

She loved him more at that moment than she ever had. She moved close and nuzzled her face into his shoulder, letting one arm drape lazily over his bare chest. ''Will you wear a ring, too?''

''If you like.''

''Of course I like,'' she muttered, sliding her head back to glare up at him. ''I don't want other women thinking you're available. My gosh, competition is fierce these days.''

''As if you'd have to worry about that,'' he mused, letting his eyes drop deliberately to her bare torso. ''Whew! Would you mind putting your clothes back on? Honestly, I've never seen anything so brazen. Tearing off your blouse, forcing me to kiss your—''

"Stop it!" she gasped, leaping to her feet. "Shame on you!"

He watched her, relaxed, delighted, while she struggled with clips and buttons. "Hussy," he accused.

She glared at him. "You just hold your breath until I take my blouse off for you again, you unappreciative peasant," she told him.

He got to his feet, rubbing his thigh gingerly, and pulled his own shirt back on. "Aren't we supposed to go to work today?" he asked.

She gasped, running to find a clock. "It's nine-thirty!" she exclaimed. "We're an hour late."

"My, my, we did spend some time lying down, didn't we?" he murmured, grinning at her blush. "What a pity we aren't already married... Speaking of that, we'll get the license and the blood tests this morning, and next week we can put the wedding in the paper. We'll get Jess and Judy to be witnesses, Kelly can give you away. We'll let old preacher Barnes marry us in the Presbyterian church...." He glanced at Wynn, who was feeling shell-shocked by the speed with which he was planning. "You're still Presbyterian?" And when she nodded in a dazed way, he continued, "And we can be married Saturday. Okay?"

She was still nodding, feeling her whole life pass before her eyes.

"Come on, before you freeze in that position," he said, taking her arm. "We've got a lot of loose ends to tie up. Move, darling."

She followed him out the door. Those few days went by in an incredible rush. It was Friday afternoon, the blood tests were over, the license was in McCabe's pocket, the ceremony was set for ten a.m. the next morning, and Wynn was staring at a wall in the office trying to imagine being married to McCabe. He'd gone off to a civic-club luncheon and hadn't returned, but he'd been muttering something about going with the mayor to a budget meeting, so he was probably going to be late. She smiled, thinking about how it had been between them. He'd kissed her, but there had been no repeats of that wild interlude on the couch. She missed the startling newness of being caressed by him, but the waiting wasn't all that hard. Not when she could see the light at the end of the tunnel and it was rainbow-bright. One more night alone in her bed, and then...

She sighed. Yes, she'd have him, physically. But when would he decide to leave for Central America? He was still technically employed by the wire service; he couldn't prolong his leave of absence once he was healed, not if he wanted to continue in the job. Not even when Wynn could see the love he'd never yet stated in his eyes. He cared. He just didn't care quite enough.

The sudden trill of the telephone caught her off guard, and she picked it up.

"Redvale *Courier.* Wynn Ascot speaking."

"Just the girl," said one of the women she knew from the drugstore. "Listen, do you know what's going on over at the cotton gin? Police cars are swarming around here like crazy, and old Mike Hamm said he heard they'd cornered an escaped murderer over there. Is there anything on your scanner?''

Wynn caught her breath. ''I'll see.'' She ran to turn on the scanner, and immediately caught some coded messages, very urgent, between the local police and the sheriff's department. Sure enough, they mentioned the gin, and two suspects.

Wynn picked up the phone. ''The scanner said there were two,'' she murmured.

There was something muffled, then the woman's voice again. ''That was Ben, with the fire department—I ran out and caught him as he went by the door. He said it's two escaped murderers from the prison in Reidsville. One of them had family south of here. The police stopped the stolen car and Randy Turner's been shot.''

''Randy!'' Wynn knew him, he was a young man with a wife and baby who'd been with the police department only six months. ''How is he?''

''Bad. They don't know if he'll live. Ben thought he heard them say they'd made an arrest. Thank God, can you imagine—''

"I'd better get over there before it's all over, if I want my pix," Wynn interrupted. "Thanks for the tip! That's one I owe you!"

"Anytime."

Wynn grabbed up her camera and stuck a pad and pen in her purse. "Be back soon," she called to Judy. "They've just arrested a couple of escaped murderers at the gin!"

"Be careful!" Judy called after her.

"I'm always careful," she called back. It was only a block to the gin, so she left the car at the office and started running. A car would only get in the way, anyhow.

She knew a back way to the gin, so she took it, weaving down an alley toward the metal building, which was deserted now that peanuts and soybeans were the main crop instead of cotton.

Her skirts flew as she turned the corner...and found herself suddenly, sickeningly, in front of a leveled pistol, held by one of two badly dressed men coming straight down the alley toward her.

Chapter Ten

Wynn stopped dead, staring helplessly at the pistol, which seemed to be ten times life size. She could see the darkness inside the barrel and wondered frantically if this was it.

"A broad!" the taller man exclaimed. "Talk about the luck of the Irish," he added in a Northern accent. "Get her by the arm, Tony. Now we got some bargaining power."

"You're the answer to a prayer, lady," the dark, foreign-looking man called Tony said, taking her arm roughly. "Now, don't you cause no trouble, and you won't get hurt. You just come right along with Jack and Tony and don't make no trouble.''

The hand gripping her so tightly was shaking. Both men were flushed and sweating wildly, and she could smell their fear. Or was it her own? she wondered, forcing her numb legs to move. Oh, McCabe, she thought miserably, why didn't I listen to you?

The shorter man thrust her hand behind her, angrily dislodging the camera and purse from her shoulder and slamming them to the ground. ''Now, hold still, lady!'' he growled.

''Hey, fuzz!'' the taller man yelled as the three of them pressed against the corner of the building where the alley led to the street.

The police chief stood up behind his car. ''What do you want?''

Wynn recognized Bill Davis, one of the finest officers the town had ever produced and, fortunately, one well-trained in bargaining. The relief Wynn felt was overwhelming, because there were younger men on the force who were a little less patient.

''We picked up a passenger,'' the tall man yelled. ''A lady. With a big camera.''

"Wynn!" Bill burst out.

"That your name, lady?" Tony asked sharply, forcing her arm back farther until it felt as if it would snap. "Does he know you?"

"Yes," she gasped. "I'm a reporter."

"By God," the taller man burst out, "just what we need. Okay, honey, you just keep cool and you'll get the story of your life."

"Will I live to tell it?" she asked.

"Maybe, if you do right." The tall man raised his voice. "That's her name, fuzz, she's a reporter. Now, you just do like I say and she won't get hurt."

"What do you want, Mooney?" Chief Davis called sharply, and Wynn heard the concern in his voice and hated her own stupidity for making the situation worse.

"I want a helicopter," he called back. "And a pilot to fly us anywhere I say."

There was a pause and voices rumbling. "Mooney, the closest one we can get belongs to the Army. We'll have to send to the base for it—it will take time."

"I got no time," the escapee yelled back, "and neither has this broad!"

"I can't get a chopper in less than two hours!" Davis called back. "But there's a light aircraft at the airport, the pilot's right here. He says he'll take you up."

The two men looked at each other. "What do you think, Jack?" the foreign-looking one asked urgently. "The longer we stay here, the hotter it's gonna get. They'll bring in more fuzz and pretty soon they might decide to rush us. We got no choice!"

"I don't know," Jack said gruffly. "Maybe it's a trap. I don't trust these local yokels."

Wynn was hoping she wouldn't faint or give in to the panic she felt. The gun was at her throat and she wanted to scream and cry and beg for her life, but these men were desperate enough not to care if they had to kill her, and she knew it. She could taste death as she never had, and the only thought in her mind was that she might never see McCabe again.

"Wait a minute," the taller one said, glaring at Wynn. "She knows that local fuzz. Hey, broad, you tell me if he's on the level. Put that gun a little closer, Tony, make her real nervous. Come on, broad, is he a square john?''

She swallowed. "Yes," she managed on a broken sob. "His word is his honor, he won't break it. He won't...let anyone else break it, either."

The taller man relaxed a little, but the gun pressed harder against her throat.

"Maybe we could take her with us," the shorter one said. "Yeah, Jack, we can take her along!"

Jack nodded. "Okay," he said with sudden decision.

The gun moved away, and although she was still held painfully by the escapee, she breathed just a bit easier.

"Okay, fuzz, we'll take the plane," the convict yelled at the policemen. "But the broad comes with us. Now, we're coming out. My buddy's got a gun in her back. At the first unexpected move, she's gonna die fast. You got that, fuzz?"

"I understand," Bill Davis said calmly. "Come on out, Mooney, nobody's going to fire.'' He yelled to his men to put away their weapons.

And then the longest walk of Wynn's life began. It was only half a block to the road. But each step was an agony of fear and anticipation. What if the man's finger slipped, what if he stumbled? The pistol barrel was cold and hard in the small of her back, and she was trembling so much it was an effort to walk. She knew there were tears running down her cheeks, but she couldn't help it. She was utterly terrified.

Nothing existed in the whole world except the expanse of concrete under her feet and the gun at her back. She was aware of the discomfort of her arm being bent back behind her, the footsteps of the men who held her prisoner. In the distance she made out uniforms and flashing blue lights.

Her mind was running wild, but Wynn forced herself to think calmly. If they took her out of Redvale, her chances of getting away alive were nil. They'd kill the pilot and her, too. With murder convictions behind them, two more murders wouldn't matter at all. She had to think, and fast. The taller man wasn't carrying a gun. Only the short one was armed. That would make things a little easier, if she could manage some way to help the police get the drop on them without getting herself or some innocent person shot in the process.

She could faint, but the convict would simply hold on to her, or shoot her on the way down, and she'd have accomplished nothing. The men were nervous, wildly nervous, and she understood. She was nervous, too. The threat of being shot and killed was enough to make anyone shake.

"Jack," the shorter one exclaimed huskily as they approached the crowd around the police car. "Jack, what if they—"

"Shut up!" the taller one snapped. "Don't lose your nerve, you dummy. And watch the girl. These idiot reporters don't mind taking chances."

"Sure, Jack." He pushed the gun barrel punishingly against her spine. "Feel this, lady? I'll blow you in half if you try anything, you got that?"

"I wouldn't…dream of it," she ground out. Her arm felt as if it were being jerked out of the socket, but she was still working on ways and means of escape.

The men jerked her out onto the sidewalk, and the first person Wynn saw, standing rigidly beside Bill Davis, was McCabe!

He was leaning heavily on the cane, his face a mask that she couldn't see behind, somber and stern and unyielding.

"This is the pilot," Davis said, nodding at McCabe. "He'll fly you out."

"You got a license, man?" the taller of the escapees asked McCabe.

"Don't worry," McCabe said with a mocking smile. "I can fly it."

"Well, you don't try nothing funny, or the girl gets it," the shorter convict told him. "Let's go."

McCabe limped forward on the cane, and Wynn's eyes widened, saying things he didn't seem to see. His eyes were on the two men and they didn't waver as he came close.

"That's far enough, man," the one called

Tony rasped, tightening his hold on Wynn. He cocked the gun. "You hear that? I'll kill her if you come any closer!"

The taller man was looking terrified. "Stay back, I tell you!"

McCabe stopped just in front of Wynn. "Now, boys," he said calmly, "what's the matter? Nobody's going to shoot. You just let the lady go, and I'll be your hostage. Okay?"

Wynn held her breath. The two escapees looked at each other nervously.

"He's a big one," Tony muttered.

"Yeah, but he's crippled, see how he's leaning on that cane?" the one called Jack muttered. "Hell, it'll be easier just watching one of them. Let the girl go, and we'll take him."

McCabe's eyes were boring into the smaller man's. "That's right," he said, watching as the convict began to ease his grip on Wynn's arm, and his voice was almost hypnotic. "That's right, just let her go."

The one called Tony loosened his grip and finally released her altogether, freeing her from the painful hold and the distasteful intimacy all at once. But she didn't move. She stood exactly where she had been and watched with eyes full of horror. What if they shot McCabe, for God's sake!

But McCabe was as calm as if he'd gone fishing, despite the tiny bit of pallor that Wynn, knowing him, detected.

"Now, you don't try nothing, big boy," the short convict muttered hoarsely, and he leveled the pistol at McCabe.

McCabe gave it a hard stare, and Wynn knew he was remembering another time, another place. She wanted to scream at him to be careful, that she'd die if anything happened to him, but she was frozen in place, numb.

"He ain't gonna try nothing," the taller man said with a sarcastic grin. "Are you, big man? You're just a cripple."

"That's been said about one time too many," McCabe growled in a dangerously soft voice. And before anyone realized what that tone meant, he moved. Quickly, as if his leg were in mint condition, he shot forward, grabbing the smaller man's arm to jerk him forward. McCabe's massive fist connected with a crunch. The foreign man cried out and sank to the ground, leaving the pistol behind in McCabe's hand. He swung backward without even looking, slamming the pistol barrel straight into the face of the second convict and sending him reeling into the arms of the police. It happened so fast that Wynn's eyes blinked incredulously. And the look on McCabe's impassive face was as calm as milk in a bowl, until he turned his head and she got a look at his eyes.

"My God, you're quick!" Bill Davis exclaimed, moving forward while his men got the groggy convicts to their feet and marched them off to patrol cars. The police chief took off his hat and wiped his sweaty brow. "That was a terrible chance you took, McCabe!"

"Before you explode, look at this." McCabe broke open the chamber of the police special the convict had carried and showed it to Davis.

"Empty!" the policeman burst out. He said

a word Wynn wouldn't have repeated and whirled. "Hey, boys, the gun was empty!"

"Well, you told me they'd fired at you several times," McCabe told him. "And when the little guy pointed it at me, I could see inside the cylinder. Assuming that there wasn't a bullet in the firing chamber, the piece was empty. But," he added with a grim smile, "the look in the man's eyes told me he was bluffing. That was all I needed."

"I thought you'd gone nuts," Davis admitted, studying him. "What if the gun had been loaded?"

"I'd be dead," he said simply. He was staring at Wynn, his eyes blazing, glittering. "Are you all right?" he asked in a deep, husky tone.

She swallowed and nodded. Her lips were dry and she felt as if she were going to faint any minute. Her legs were so wobbly they barely held her up. The numbness was just beginning to wear off and she realized with startling impact how close she'd come to dying.

McCabe drew in a long, slow breath. "I could have killed them both," he said heavily.

"I could have killed them for putting you through that."

"I'm all right," she said weakly, and managed a smile. "Sorry I got in the way, Bill. I thought they said you'd made an arrest."

"Never trust a rumor, don't you know that?" Davis said patiently. He shook his head and whistled through his lips. "That was close. I was going to stall for time and bargain. If that didn't work, I was going to risk a rush. But McCabe happened along at just the right moment. Son, I guess hopping around trouble spots does give you an edge. I won't even mention how Mooney's jaw got cracked," he added with a smile.

McCabe glanced at him. "If he wants to press charges, I'd be delighted to go to court with him," he said. "Tell him I said that."

"I don't think he's going to be too anxious to make trouble. He's in enough as it is." He patted Wynn on the back. "Stick to reporting and leave catching crooks to us, will you, Wynn? You're just plain rotten at this."

"Sure, Bill," she said shakily, and grinned. "Next time, I'll stay by the scanner."

"Thanks a lot," he called over his shoulder. "You'll need to come down to the station and sign a statement."

"Let me get my knees calmed down and I'll be right with you," she said.

The police cars roared away, and a crowd gathered to see what the commotion was. Taking advantage of the uproar, McCabe took Wynn's arm and escorted her back down the alley to the office while nobody was looking. He was grim and unsmiling, and his eyes were frightening.

"What happened?" Judy asked excitedly. Kelly and Jess turned, listening from the back, where they were working.

"Later," McCabe said curtly. He took Wynn into the office and slammed the door behind them.

"Now, McCabe," she began, feeling too shaken for an argument.

But he wasn't arguing. He pulled her into his arms and held her as if he were afraid she might get away. His face burrowed into her throat and he breathed roughly. The arms holding her trembled, his body trembled. He groaned, and held her even closer.

"Oh, God," he ground out huskily. "Oh, God…oh, God, I've never been so afraid in all my life!"

She smoothed the hair at the nape of his strong neck, running her fingers through it lightly, tenderly. "It's all right, darling," she whispered softly. "I'm fine, really I am…just a little shaky. They didn't hurt me. I'm only bruised a little."

He was still shaking, and it frightened her to see him like this, to see him so vulnerable and upset.

"McCabe, I'm all right," she repeated, holding him, clinging to him. "I'm all right!"

"If that gun had been loaded," he said in a strained, harsh tone, "I could have lost you. Right there, on the street, with a dozen policemen watching, I could have had to watch you die."

"But you didn't," she said softly. "And a miss is as good as a mile, isn't it?"

"No, it damned well isn't!" He took in a

sharp breath and lifted his head. His face was paper white, his eyes filled with raw emotion. "That's it. That's all. You're quitting. You're going to go home and have babies and raise roses! But you're not going to work here."

Her eyes widened. "It's my job!"

"It was," he said coldly. "Not anymore."

"Why? Because of a once-in-a-million incident that ended without tragedy?" she demanded. "You won't give up your job, why should I?"

He stood there staring at her, and all the expression drained out of his face. Every last bit of it. "This is how you felt when I told you how I got shot, isn't it?" he asked slowly, with dawning realization. "This...sickening coldness is just exactly what you felt."

She nodded. "Just exactly."

He took a deep breath and his hands moved warmly up and down her arms. He studied her pale face with eyes that worshiped every soft line of it, every curve, every crevice.

"Well," he sighed heavily, "I guess I'd

better get some information on the water situation in south Georgia. Harry's going to need a lot of help to get the message across to the voters when they call a referendum on the countrywide water system this fall.''

Tears sprang up like green fountains in her eyes and she stared at him uncomprehendingly.

''You'll have to be patient at first, of course,'' he continued, unabashed. ''If I start wearing bush shirts and carrying a machete in the backyard, you'll have to pretend it's perfectly normal. And if I wear my pith helmet to work once in a while, you mustn't stare.''

She nodded, teeth biting her lip, trying to take it all in after the emotional experience she'd been through.

''And you'll have to be patient about consummating the marriage, because this leg is killing me!'' he groaned, moving it restlessly.

''McCabe, I...'' She was feeling guilty now about all that he was giving up. ''I think maybe I could get used to it.''

''Well, I couldn't,'' he said flatly, jerking

her close and wincing when his leg collided
with hers. He eased it between hers, and lifted
an eyebrow when she flushed at the intimate
contact. "My, my, this is an interesting position, isn't it?" he murmured.

"Will you listen to me?"

"I'm trying. But you're stumbling all over
the place, darling." He bent and took her
mouth softly, slowly. "Your legs are trembling," he breathed into her open mouth.

"Well, so are yours," she laughed huskily.

He lifted his head and glanced at the desk
and raised an eyebrow. She blushed red and
hit his chest.

"It was only a thought," he murmured,
smiling as he bent again.

"I don't want my first time to be on somebody's desk," she muttered.

"It would be my first time, too," he told
her. "I only write those erotic scenes, Wynn,
I don't live them. I don't have any notion
about how you'd do it, but I'm perfectly willing to experiment in the name of science."

She burst out laughing and ruffled his thick

hair lovingly. "You'd be screaming because of your leg," she assured him.

"Remember what I told you about that?" he murmured, brushing his mouth over her face warmly, softly. "That I could walk naked into a forest fire…"

"First," she murmured, "help Harry get the water system."

He laughed as his mouth burrowed into hers. And then the laughing stopped altogether, and they both went up in flames.

They spent their wedding night in a luxurious motel on a Florida beach, McCabe having coaxed Ed back home early for the occasion of their wedding. It had been a small one, and Wynn's dress hadn't been exactly what she wanted, because there wasn't a lot of choice on such short notice. But it was the most beautiful wedding she'd ever been to, and she felt absurdly feminine with McCabe's proud eyes on her through the entire ceremony.

She lay in his arms on the balcony in the large chair he'd pulled out there, and watched the whitecaps hit the moonlit beach. They'd just finished supper in their room, and he'd tugged her down into his lap so that she was lying across his good leg and not putting pressure on the bad one.

"Are you comfortable?" she asked.

"Of course not. Now, shut up. I'm trying to kiss you."

"In that case..." She smiled as his mouth found hers in the dim light, and sighed. "Oh, McCabe, I wish we had the beach to ourselves and that you were in peak condition."

"Why?" he murmured, bending his head to nudge aside the low-cut blouse she was wearing and trespass on warm, silky skin.

"I'd like to lie on the beach with you."

"Hmm," he laughed, "and I can imagine in what circumstances. But, Wynn, think of the sand!"

"We could take a towel with us," she said, pouting. "Anyway, I know you aren't able—"

"That's what you think, lady." He lifted her up and tugged her back into the room, pausing to turn down the double bed without turning on the light. He tugged off his clothes while she gaped at him, chuckling when he was through and she was still frozen in position.

He came close, removing her blouse and the rest of her comfortable outfit until she felt the cool ocean breeze on her bareness with an incredible sense of freedom.

"Now," he said, lifting her and tossing her into the center of the bed, "just pretend that this is sand, and the sheet is a towel, and close your eyes. I'll take care of the rest."

She opened her mouth to protest, but he was already sliding alongside her, and she caught her breath on a wild, husky little moan as she felt for the first time in her life the silky roughness of a man's bare flesh against every inch of her own.

"McCabe," she moaned.

"You need to learn some new words," he whispered in her ear as his hands made new, exciting discoveries about her. "Before morning, you'll have a great vocabulary."

He was a patient lover. And he knew where

to touch, how to arouse gently, how not to frighten. She found herself obeying his soft, tender whispers without a single protest as he led her deeper and deeper into a morass of sensuality that surpassed even her wild imaginings about being with him.

He whispered words in Spanish and taught her the meanings, and then taught her to repeat them. He calmed her last helpless surge of fear and gentled her, cradled her, until the wildness of passion caught her and tossed her up against him like the pulsating whitecaps that lashed the beach. And the pain was hardly beginning before it ended, and she went with him every step of the way, his willing companion in a journey of exploration that ended all too soon.

She nestled in his arms, still shaking with mingled pleasure and frustration, because it had been exquisite but not nearly enough.

"It gets better," he murmured wickedly when he had his breath back. He brushed his lips over her closed eyes. "Much, much better. But it takes a lot of practice, so you'll just have to eat a lot and conserve your strength."

"You're just impossible," she burst out, laughing.

"I always have been. Seriously, was it good at all?" he asked gently.

"It was extremely intimate," she murmured. "Oh, McCabe, I love you so much. I'm just so glad that you're not going to be risking your life anymore."

"That goes double for me, darling," he said flatly. "I've got so much to live for now. I'll never forget the terror I felt when it dawned on me that you were my whole world and if anything happened to you, I might as well let them shoot me, too. Because I wouldn't want to live if I had to do it without you."

She caught her breath at the genuine emotion in his deep voice as he spoke. In the dimness she could see the flash of his eyes.

"I love you, Wynn," he said curtly. "All the way."

"I knew that already," she said unsteadily. "But it's very nice to hear it."

"You've said it quite a lot," he murmured, drawing her back down beside him. "While I was teaching you how to make love. Feel up to another lesson so soon?"

"Oh, yes," she whispered with a laugh. "If you do."

"I'll manage." He lifted her over him and laughed when she gasped. "Remember when I told you there are ways, and ways? Well, this is what I meant."

She caught her breath and let him pull her down into the maelstrom with him. And this time, it was enough. More than enough. It was all the world and every nuance of love it contained. He was hers. And she was his. Totally.

A long time later, they ordered coffee and pie from room service and sat together in the big chair on the balcony.

"McCabe, about your job," she began uneasily. "Will you be able to settle for what Redvale can offer?"

"I've thought about that a lot," he said. "And I think I can, Wynn. As long as you don't mind traveling with me once in a while. I want to climb the ruins at Machu Picchu and on Crete and see the pyramids. I'd like to go around the world without being obligated to report what I see. Would you like that?''

"Yes, I would.'' She nuzzled closer. "And when our children get old enough, we'll take them with us.''

"How many are we going to have?'' he asked on a chuckle.

"Well, I thought maybe a boy and a girl.''

"Nice. We'll teach them how to handle a camera and write choppy sentences.'' He kissed her nose. "Will you miss it a lot?''

"No more than you will, I guess,'' she admitted.

"Wynn, Ed made me a proposition,'' he said after a minute.

"What kind of proposition?''

"He offered me the paper.''

She sat up, holding her breath. "And?''

He studied her. "How would you like to run it with me?''

"Oh, McCabe!'' she burst out, laughing, loving him. "McCabe, what a nice wedding present!''

He drew her close and kissed her. "I'm still

working on the roomful of roses.'' He eased her back down into his arms. ''Now, this is how I thought we'd start out,'' he began. And she nuzzled closer, smiling a little as she listened. It might not be easy to get this tiger into a permanent cage, but now that he had a wife and a newspaper of his own, he might settle down quite well. She lifted her hand to his face, and her wedding ring caught the moonlight. It was no more radiant than Wynn's eyes, with the glow of fulfillment blazing softly in their depths.

A showgirl, a minister—
and an unsolved murder.

EASY VIRTUE

Eight years ago Mary Margaret's father was
convicted of a violent murder she knew he
didn't commit—and she vowed to clear his
name. With her father serving a life sentence,
Mary Margaret is working as a showgirl in Reno
when Reverend Dane Barrett shows up with
information about her father's case. Working to
expose the real killer, the unlikely pair also
proceed to expose themselves to an unknown
enemy who is intent on keeping the past buried.

**From the bestselling author of
LAST NIGHT IN RIO**

JANICE KAISER

Available in December 1997
at your favorite retail outlet.

Take 3 of "The Best of the Best™" Novels FREE
Plus get a FREE surprise gift!

Special Limited-time Offer
Mail to The Best of the Best™

3010 Walden Avenue
P.O. Box 1867
Buffalo, N.Y. 14240-1867

YES! Please send me 3 free novels and my free surprise gift. Then send me 3 of "The Best of the Best™" novels each month. I'll receive the best books by the world's hottest romance authors. Bill me at the low price of $3.99 each plus 25¢ delivery per book and applicable sales tax, if any.* That's the complete price and a savings of over 20% off the cover prices—quite a bargain! I understand that accepting the books and gift places me under no obligation ever to buy any books. I can always return a shipment and cancel at any time. Even if I never buy another book, the 3 free books and the surprise gift are mine to keep forever.

183 BPA A4V9

Name	(PLEASE PRINT)	
Address	Apt. No.	
City	State	Zip

This offer is limited to one order per household and not valid to current subscribers.
*Terms and prices are subject to change without notice. Sales tax applicable in N.Y. All orders subject to approval.

BARBARA DELINSKY

New York Times Bestselling Author!

Sasha was a romance writer—but she couldn't have *created* a scene any better...

SASHA BLAKE met him by accident—literally. She crashed her motorcycle into his sports car. But she must have hit her head harder than she thought, because he looked exactly like the hero from her latest novel.

DOUG DONOHUE—handsome, kind and caring—was just too good to be true. But there had to be a catch. He wasn't a hero from one of her novels—and how could he live up to her expectations?

Bronze Mystique

"Women's fiction at its finest."—*Romantic Times*

Available in December 1997 at your favorite retail outlet.

MIRA BOOKS

The Brightest Stars in Women's Fiction.™

Look us up on-line at: http://www.romance.net

MBD423

MURDER, BLACKMAIL AND LIES...

Suspicion

A young law clerk is killed. A high-priced call girl is strangled. Two men are accused of their murders. And defense attorney Kate Logan intends to prove their innocence—even though the evidence and witnesses say otherwise. With the help of homicide detective Mitch Calhoun, Kate discovers evidence suggesting that the two cases may be connected. But when her life and the life of her daughter are threatened, Kate and Mitch realize they have stumbled into a maze of corruption and murder...where no one is above suspicion.

CHRISTIANE HEGGAN

"A master at creating taut, romantic suspense." –*Literary Times*

Good Girls

When they were good...

Suzanne, Taylor and Annie:
three Southern women whose lives are
tainted by one man—the charismatic,
ruthlessly ambitious Jack Sullivan—until
he's finally stopped by a bullet.

Welcome to the Old South—
where even good girls turn bad.

Karen Young

Available in January 1998—
where books are sold.

 **The Brightest Stars
in Women's Fiction.™**

162

From the bestselling author of *Jury Duty*

Laura Van Wormer

It's New York City's most sought-after address—a prestigious boulevard resplendent with majestic mansions and impressive apartments. But hidden behind the beauty and perfection of this neighborhood, with its wealthy and famous residents, are the often destructive forces of lies and secrets, envy and undeniable temptations.

Step on to...

RIVERSIDE DRIVE

MIRA BOOKS

Available in January 1998—
where books are sold.

MLVW303